"Stop right there

"And if I don't?" he ask

She didn't immediately ~~~~~~ being bold, challenging her. Not exactly the actions of someone guilty. But still... Either way, this guy could be trampling on evidence.

"I'm Detective Cordon," she relented, leaving off the bit about being a newly minted detective. "Identify yourself now or they'll do it for you at Tarrant County Jail."

He turned around and she nodded toward the badge clipped to the waistline of her jogging pants.

His eyes lingered there a little longer than she was comfortable with and heat flushed her cheeks.

"Deacon Kent," he said. Why did that name sound familiar?

"Do you have any knowledge of the crime committed here last night?" she pressed.

"Only what I read in the *Fort Worth Star-Telegram* this morning." His voice was calm.

"The *Telegram* reports on crime every day. You show up at every crime scene?" she asked him.

He hesitated in answering and that meant one thing.

Deacon Kent was hiding something.

AMBUSHED AT CHRISTMAS

USA TODAY Bestselling Author

BARB HAN

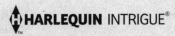

All my love to Brandon, Jacob and Tori, my favorite people in the world.

To Babe, my hero, for being my great love and my place to call home.

ISBN-13: 978-1-335-64125-0

Ambushed at Christmas

Copyright © 2019 by Barb Han

Recycling programs for this product may not exist in your area.

Printed in U.S.A.

™ www.Harlequin.com

USA TODAY bestselling author **Barb Han** lives in north Texas with her very own hero-worthy husband, three beautiful children, a spunky golden retriever/standard poodle mix and too many books in her to-read pile. In her downtime, she plays video games and spends much of her time on or around a basketball court. She loves interacting with readers and is grateful for their support. You can reach her at barbhan.com.

Books by Barb Han

Harlequin Intrigue

Rushing Creek Crime Spree

Cornered at Christmas
Ransom at Christmas
Ambushed at Christmas

Crisis: Cattle Barge

Sudden Setup
Endangered Heiress
Texas Grit
Kidnapped at Christmas
Murder and Mistletoe
Bulletproof Christmas

Cattlemen Crime Club

Stockyard Snatching
Delivering Justice
One Tough Texan
Texas-Sized Trouble
Texas Witness
Texas Showdown

Harlequin Intrigue Noir

Atomic Beauty

Visit the Author Profile page at Harlequin.com.

CAST OF CHARACTERS

Leah Cordon—This homicide detective jogs into the trap of a murderer.

Deacon Kent—This Kent brother will stop at nothing to find out who is butchering heifers on his family's ranch.

Detective Charles Dougherty—This coworker doesn't appreciate the way Leah ended their fling and lets his frustration show every time their professional paths cross.

Nick Chester—Was this witness at the wrong place at the wrong time? Or is he involved in murder?

Elijah Henry—Much like the perp everyone's looking for, Elijah has a limp and seems to have a reason not to like women. But is he responsible for murder?

Zach McWilliams—A fine lawman who has to stand on the sidelines and cooperate with a crime that occurs outside his jurisdiction and impacts his family.

Chapter One

Homicide Detective Leah Cordon jogged along the familiar path of the Trinity River Trail in Fort Worth, Texas. She was halfway through her run and a cold front had arrived, causing a frigid gust of wind to penetrate the terry hoodie she wore.

December weather in Texas could drop from high sixty-degree temperatures to well below freezing in half an hour. She pushed her pace to increase her heart rate in order to stave off the next couple of blasts.

Leah reached up to tug on the rubber band taming her normally unruly locks and freed her hair from a ponytail in hopes that it would provide a little extra insulation. The loose-fitting hood wouldn't stay put so she didn't bother pulling it over her head. Instead, she zipped her lightweight vest up to the neck. She didn't like the idea of blocking access to her Glock, which was something she hadn't considered needing on her nightly run until a woman had been murdered near this very spot last night.

At ten o'clock the sky was covered with rolling gray clouds, blocking out all moonlight. She was entering the stretch of trail where trees thickened and there was little artificial light.

"Bad Medicine" by Bon Jovi rocked through her left earbud. She always kept one ear clear in order to listen for faster runners, bikers or in-line skaters. Fatalities with pedestrians who were distracted by earbuds and cell phones were rising at a dizzying pace, especially at intersections. But now she felt the need to listen for a predator.

Leah tugged at her covered thumbholes to hold her sleeves in place over her base layer.

Keeping her pace, she considered turning back for a split second as the exact spot that the woman was pulled off the trail last night and brutally murdered came into focus. Crime scene tape roped off the section of trees where she'd been found fifteen feet off the trail.

A dozen temporarily placed lamps illuminated the path ahead.

The feeling of eyes watching her pricked the hairs on the back of her neck. A cold chill raced down her spine. She blamed it on the cold front, the area. Even so, the creepy feeling took hold.

Looking ahead, a yellow haze from the streetlamp covered a fifteen-foot radius. She stood outside its glow, breath coming in rasps. She reached into her pocket and pulled out her cell, turning down the volume.

Leaves rustled just ahead. Movement seemed too deep in the underbrush to be caused by gusting winds. They'd died down for the moment.

Leah stopped, pulled out the left earbud and studied the area as best she could in the dim light. Her eyes had adjusted to the dark enough to see decently. More movement ramped up her pulse. She immediately unzipped her lightweight vest in case quick access to her weapon was needed. And then a single low-hanging tree branch rustled. Her eyes tracked the movement. Her heart stuttered and her hand came up to rest on the butt of the Glock holstered inside her vest.

A rabbit scrambled out of the brush, caught eyes with her for a second and then darted off in the opposite direction.

That bunny had really gotten her heart going. Leah breathed a sigh of relief, loosening her grip on the handle.

Normally, on this stretch of trail she would've long since hit her stride and whizzed past without giving her surroundings much thought. Her police training had taught her to observe her environment but last night's homicide had her second-guessing being on this trail in the first place.

She'd be damned if she let her fears rule. Her

mind tried to flash back to the past but she forced it on the path ahead. She might not have been able to control what had happened in her youth but she could decide her focus now. She searched the area one more time before replacing her left earbud, drowning out her racing thoughts with the heavy drumbeat and raucous guitar threads.

Tucking her chin to her chest, she balled her fists and started off again. This time, she ignored the eyes-on-her shiver pricking her skin and pushed her legs harder. Running into the spot of last night's attack was most likely the reason for her case of the heebie-jeebies. An innocent bunny had caused her to jump nearly out of her skin. What would be next? A squirrel?

The sound of footsteps behind her caused her heart to stutter again. She whirled around, running backward a few steps in time to see another jogger. His hood was on, his chin to his chest, and his gait had military precision. A pair of white cords bounced in front of his hoodie that combined into one string midway down his chest.

The runner glanced up, gave a slight wave and then increased his speed until he passed her. The squirrels weren't getting to her but other runners were. Leah gave herself a mental head shake. Keep it up and she'd have to abandon her late-night runs until she could get her act together.

Stats kept spinning through Leah's mind despite the loud music thumping in her left ear. Jillian Mitchell, the victim, was five feet seven inches tall. So was Leah.

Jillian Mitchell had espresso-brown hair that had been in a ponytail last night. Same as Leah.

Jillian Mitchell had a runner's build, meaning she was pretty much all legs. Just like Leah. The killer had severed her right ankle before dragging her into the bushes.

The flashback to high school when Leah's best friend had been brutally murdered edged into her thoughts. Leah was supposed to sneak out to meet up. She'd fallen asleep instead. The crime had rocked their exclusive white-collar Arlington Heights neighborhood.

Forcing her thoughts to the present, to the trail, she was grateful that lights had been set up in the normally dark stretch known as Porter's Bend for the curvy pathway. That was a comfort. Leah tried to reestablish her pace. She had almost cleared the winding patch when she caught a glimpse of a man crouching near the brush. He was at the edge of the crime scene tape area and down on all fours. Even at this distance Leah could see that he had substantial size.

Leah slowed to a walk but her heart pounded her ribs as though she'd turned up her speed. She assessed the situation and quickly realized there was no one else around. She bit back a curse as she palmed her cell. She started to fire off a text to dispatch, noting a suspicious person at the scene of Porter's Bend.

A mix of adrenaline and fear shot through her. Had the murderer returned to the crime scene? Was the person who'd attacked and murdered Jillian Mitchell digging in the shrubs?

Reason argued against the notion. Only an idiot would come back this soon. The criminal who'd murdered Jillian didn't strike Leah as stupid. He had to know tensions were running high after last night's attack. People would be on the lookout for anyone or anything suspicious in the area and along the trail. Those were the reasons she'd used when she'd convinced herself to stick to her nightly routine and go on the run.

If she'd been on time last night, it could've been her in the morgue and not Jillian Mitchell, a little voice in the back of her head stated. She couldn't use rock music to block out the voice now.

Leah's fingers were as cold as ice cubes thanks to the frigid air. She flexed and released them a couple of times before placing her hand on the butt of her still-holstered weapon. She'd stick around until an officer arrived.

Confronting this guy without backup would be taking an unnecessary risk. Leah decided it would be best to put enough distance between them to stay out of sight. As she eased back a few steps, the man popped to his feet and wheeled around to face her.

She sidestepped behind a tree. Anything— even a tree trunk—between them would slow down a bullet if he had a gun. It might not provide complete protection but it was better than nothing.

"Hold it right there," she shouted, using the authoritative cop voice reserved for all threatening situations. "I'm a police officer. Don't take one step closer. Hands where I can see them *now*."

"I'm not moving." True to his word, he froze. His hands flew into the air, palms facing her. She scanned them for any signs of a weapon and could see that they were empty. Well, almost empty. On closer examination, he wore plastic gloves. A knot formed in her stomach, braiding her lining.

Experience had taught her that empty hands didn't mean there was no weapon present. A bullet had grazed her shin during her sophomore year as a patrol officer on a domestic violence call that had seemingly come out of nowhere. She tabled the glove-wearing part for now, careful not to reveal her suspicion that he was the Porter's Bend Killer.

"What are you doing here?" she asked, trying to steady her heart rate and keep a clear head.

"Take it easy." The man was tall. Six feet four inches if Leah had to guess. Through his unzipped denim jacket she could see that he worked out. His muscled thighs had stretched and released as he stood. His thick sandy blond hair was tightly clipped with curls at the edges. He was too far for her to see the color of his eyes but his face was all sharp angles, like the kind that looked a little too good on a billboard in a major city. He seemed familiar. Did she know him?

"What are you looking for?" she asked, trying to dig for a little more information. If he was a criminal—and specifically the one her department was looking for—the more she got him talking, the more chances he had to make a slip.

"My keys," he said. His voice was masculine. The kind that sounded like it was used to being in charge of a situation.

"What's in your front right pocket?" she asked. "I see something."

"I, uh—" He didn't glance down and that told her he knew exactly where his keys were. It wasn't uncommon for a perp to return to the scene of a crime but normally they came with search parties when the victim was missing. Jillian Mitchell had very much been found.

"Save the story." She leveled her gaze on the man. "What are you really looking for?"

"What did you say your name was?" he shot back.

"I didn't."

"Then we have nothing left to say." He turned his back to her.

There was no way she'd shoot without being provoked but this maneuver said he knew it.

"Stop right there," she warned.

"And if I don't?" he asked.

"What are the gloves for?" She used her cop voice to show him just how serious she was.

He froze.

"You better start talking here unless you want to do it downtown. We can start with your name," she continued.

"It's cold. These were all I had in the glove box," he said.

She didn't immediately answer. He was being bold, challenging her. Perhaps he was an amateur crime solver or someone hired by the Mitchell family. They had money.

Either way, this guy could be trampling on evidence.

"Detective Cordon," she relented, leaving off the bit about being a newly minted detective. She lowered her weapon. "Identify yourself now or they'll do it for you at Tarrant County Jail."

He turned around and she nodded toward the badge clipped to the waistline of her jogging pants.

His eyes lingered there a little longer than she was comfortable and heat flushed her cheeks. That was the great part about having skin the color of milk. It was near impossible to hide her emotions.

"Deacon Kent," he said. Why did that name sound familiar?

"Do you have any knowledge of the crime committed here last night?"

"Only what I read in the *Fort Worth Star Telegram* this morning." His voice was calm.

There could be benefits to publicity on a case. Leah didn't like it in this instance. Stories spawned copycats and brought out all kinds of wackos. In Mr. Kent, she saw neither and that could mean he was close to Jillian Mitchell, looking for vigilante justice.

This case set Leah's nerves on edge. The brutality of the attack made it look like a revenge killing. Not to mention this had happened on her trail. Leah matched the description of the victim, which had happened in cases before but always gave her the prickly sensation of a cat walking over a grave.

She couldn't count how many times her well-being had been threatened by jerks she'd arrested while on the job. But the thought of someone actually trying to make good didn't sit well.

"The *Telegram* reports on crime every day. You show up at every crime scene?" she asked Mr. Kent.

He hesitated in answering and that meant one thing.

Deacon Kent was hiding something.

DEACON FIGURED HE'D better come clean with the detective. The woman picked him apart with her gaze. "That's the only reason I'm here. The story in the paper. And, no, I don't show up at crime scenes uninvited."

Her brow shot up. The detective's long wavy hair—the color of richly blended coffee—fell well past her shoulders, framing a face too delicate for the badge clipped on her hip. At a little more than five and a half feet tall, wearing jogging pants that hugged a taut figure, her gaze said she was a force to be reckoned with.

"What made you come out tonight?" she asked.

He let that one go.

"I can drag you down to the station to talk if you'd be more comfortable," she said in more of a hiss.

That may be true, but Deacon wasn't doing anything wrong. He hadn't technically trespassed on a crime scene. He'd made certain not to cross the obvious area cordoned off with police tape. Even he could see that being there feeling around on the ground made him look suspicious.

"Before you get any ideas—" he paused to double-check that she wasn't a trigger-happy detective "—can I put my hands down now?"

"No. In fact, up against the tree. Hands where I can see 'em," she said, using that authoritative law enforcement voice he was all too familiar with, considering his cousin was the sheriff of Broward County. Experience had taught him not to argue with that voice and he couldn't deny that he had been crawling around in the bushes at a crime scene. He'd known getting caught would be a possibility, even though he thought he'd checked out the area well enough before dropping down on all fours.

"Okay." He kept his hands high as he walked toward the nearest tree trunk. "Let's take it easy. I'm not the guy you're looking for, so there's no need to get hysterical."

Detective Cordon issued a grunt sound.

For a split second he thought she might have been involved in a sting operation. The detective matched the basic description of the woman who'd been attacked at this very spot last night.

He glanced around for any signs of a stakeout.

But then, wouldn't another officer have made him or herself known by now?

"Do you mind telling me what *you're* doing here?" he asked, figuring it couldn't hurt.

"Right now? I'm patting you down," she countered. Her voice had a throaty note and he detected the shift in tone the moment she put her hands on him—hands that sent inappropriate sensations firing from each point of contact.

In this cold, and the temperature had dropped twenty degrees in the last fifteen minutes, he should have been shivering. Warmth shot through him and it had everything to do with the electricity coming from the detective's touch.

"I'd noticed." She'd figure it out but he decided to add, "I'm not packing heat and I don't have any other weapons."

"I'll be the judge of that." He'd expected her response to be something to that effect.

As she resumed patting him down, more annoying sensations fired up. They had no business in this situation so he ignored them.

"Turn around," she stated, using that cop voice again.

This also wasn't the time to notice the perfume she wore as he wheeled around to face her. At least, he guessed it was cologne. He'd never smelled anything like it before. If he were pressed for a description, he might have said it was like walking in the meadow after a cool spring shower with the first rays of sun hitting the land, waking the flowers.

Deacon mentally shook off the head trip.

"Keep your hands where I can see 'em." She studied him. Their gazes held for a second longer than courtesy dictated. A blush crawled across her cheeks and it was damn sexy when her cheeks flamed.

Way to stay focused.

Finished with the weapons check, she took a step back. "You're cleared."

"Like I already told you." Deacon wanted this over with so he could get back to searching the area.

"This is the scene of a murder investigation." The detective almost leveled him with her stare, which took some doing with someone as hardened as him.

"Why are you really here?"

Chapter Two

This conversation wasted valuable time. It was late. Days on the ranch started early. Deacon had often joked with his brothers and sister that he could remember a time when 4:00 a.m. was the time to end the night, not begin a day. Being a Kent was a privilege, make no mistake about it, but one that came with obligations.

Deacon figured he could tap dance around the subject with the detective all night but decided to get to the point. As far as the murder, he considered it ranch business. "That's exactly why I came, to see the crime scene."

"You taking pictures on your phone?" Disgust came through clearly as soon as she unclenched her back teeth to speak. She'd probably seen just about everything in her line of work, including crazy folks who had morbid obsessions with death and murder sites.

"Check for yourself." He gave her a look before fishing his cell from his pocket and holding it between them.

She took the offering and scrolled through his photo log. He hoped the offer would buy a little trust. Instead, as she scanned the pictures, she started rocking her head. "I know why your name sounded familiar now. Your family owns half of Texas, Wyoming and Idaho."

"That's an exaggeration." She had the states right, just not the quantity of land.

"Cattle ranchers," she continued, ignoring his comment, seeming like she was on a roll and would connect the dots as to why he was really there at any minute.

"That's right." They were cattle ranchers but owning mineral rights to their land had made his family fortune. It had also freed them from some of the pressures of cattle ranching. A bad year or a severe drought wouldn't put them out of business. It also gave them ample space to take risks and create innovation. They'd been pioneers in the organic beef market.

The puzzle pieces clicked together so loudly in the detective's mind he could almost hear them.

"You're here because of the…" She met his gaze. This close, he could see the cinnamon flecks in her eyes.

"Severed foot," he finished for her when her sentence dovetailed into silence.

"I read an article a few days ago about the heifers on your ranch turning up with severed left hooves," she continued.

"Two other ranches have called to report the same crimes. Which brings us up-to-date with why I'm here," he stated.

In a flash her expression changed. It was like she'd put in a quarter and hit all three numbers on the slot machine. "And you think the guy who's been killing cattle has moved on to people."

"Isn't that how it usually works? Don't most serial killers start with animals?" he asked.

"Yes. They usually start with something smaller, though." Detective Cordon continued to take him apart with her stare. Now she looked like she was trying to determine if he needed a trip to Golden Pond Mental Hospital.

"Found three rabbits along Rushing Creek. Carcasses had been pretty picked through and they were in advanced stages of decay, all missing a front left paw."

Now her brain really fired on all cylinders.

"I don't remember reading anything about that," she admitted. Her tone was laced with accusation.

He understood the implication. They'd just been found. Everyone on the ranch was being investigated. "The information will be out soon.

As it is, we've had our fair share of crazies popping out of the woodwork with leads. Jacobstown is a small community. People are scared. They see this as some kind of omen." He could tell by her reaction that the detective didn't like to be the one on the light side of important information.

"You'd think he'd put out a bulletin right away," she said.

"About rabbits that could have been caught in illegal traps and had their paws chopped off to free them?" Deacon issued a grunt. "The town's already in a panic over the heifers. Folks aren't used to crime. It's not like here in the city. People don't lock their doors where I'm from. Or at least they didn't used to."

"Everyone should lock their doors, Mr. Kent." She stuck his phone out between them. "A criminal could strike anywhere, anytime. They like easy marks."

Deacon chuckled. He couldn't help himself.

"What's that about?"

"Old Lady Rollick once shot at a friend of mine for sneaking onto her back porch to get a bite of one of her famous peach pies. Folks in Jacobstown can take care of themselves," he stated.

"Yeah?" she fired back. "Well, the scum I'm

used to dealing with wouldn't be sneaking onto a porch to steal dessert."

"Peach pie," he corrected.

"I reported you. A beat cop will be here any minute to investigate." The detective jerked an earbud out of her pocket and tucked it in her left ear. "If you'll excuse me, I have to finish my run."

As she made a move to take off, Deacon caught her arm.

"Can I ask you a question?" He mustered as much politeness as he could.

Her gaze held on to his hand and then lifted to his eyes. There was no amusement.

"What?"

"Why are you out here alone after what happened?"

"This is my trail," Leah said, hearing the defensiveness in her own voice. Deacon Kent's serious gray-blue eyes scrutinizing her were throwing her off-kilter. She reholstered her weapon, resting her hand on the butt for comfort and because she needed to touch something to push her reset button. Her fingers still tingled with sensations from touching the good-looking cowboy.

"You weren't scared to come out here alone after what happened last night?" It seemed like it was his turn to dig information out of her. She figured, with his connections, after one phone call from him to headquarters she'd be hauled into the chief's office to explain why she'd accused a Texas millionaire—billionaire?—of tampering with a crime scene. She hadn't specifically accused him and there was something about the cowboy—those serious eyes sure seemed honest—that almost had her believing he wouldn't play that card. But she hadn't made detective at the age of thirty by taking people for their word or letting every good-looking male off the hook.

She pulled out her earbud and stuck it in between them. "That's why I only use one earbud. Keep the other one free to listen so no one surprises me."

"But I caught you off guard and that's why your heart's still thumping. Anyone else could've done the same thing." He emphasized his point by dropping his gaze to the base of her throat, causing all kinds of heat to flush her cheeks.

"I was jogging. That's why my heart was, *is*, racing." Kent placated her by letting that little lie fly by. Being courteous must have been part of his Cowboy Code. "The path isn't that busy at this time of night. It's not rush hour. It's not isolated, either."

He shot her a look of disbelief, but she had no plans to detail out how hard she'd fought against her fears and why it was even more important to her now to face them.

"You can take those gloves off."

He did, and her traitorous heart fluttered in her chest like a schoolgirl crush when she saw there was no ring on his left-hand finger. She told herself that she was just doing her job. It was true enough. She did get paid to notice things.

"Mr. Kent—"

"Call me Deacon," he insisted.

She didn't like being informal with someone she'd considered a possible suspect a few minutes ago, but figured if she threw him a few bones, he'd walk away without a formal complaint. The other irritating part about him was how much his voice—a dark ale kind of timbre—trailed down her spine, causing tingles she didn't even want to consider. "Deacon." His first name sounded less awkward coming out of her mouth than she'd expected. That little tinge of a smile tugging at the corner of his lips almost made her feel like he enjoyed hearing it. "I can see that your intentions are good, if misguided."

He started to cut her off but she held her finger up to quiet him. The move would probably be gasoline on a fire.

Instead of flying off the handle, he smiled a smug smile, folded his arms and leaned back against the tree like they were old friends having a casual conversation. This guy was too smooth and full of contradictions. His calloused hands said he worked hard but a man with his family money wouldn't have to work a day. His tanned olive skin said he spent his days outside. He was tall and strong; she'd seen his jeans stretch against seriously muscled thighs when he walked.

Normally, sizing someone up for a threat didn't seem invasive or personal in the way being with Deacon Kent did.

"I can understand your interest in this case. However, I shouldn't need to warn you the person responsible is dangerous. You might think investigating on your own is smart, but—" A tree branch snapped a few feet away, causing her to jump. She pulled out her phone and put on the flashlight app before bringing the light to a small brush.

Deacon was already investigating. He'd covered the distance between them and the brush in seconds. He was fast.

Leah swept the area and then moved behind him.

"It's nothing. Animals," he said, sitting back on his heels. His hands were on his knees when he turned his head.

A scream split the air.

Deacon hopped to his feet and started toward

the cry for help as Leah darted to his side. She'd drawn her gun and was sweeping the area from side to side with it as she tore toward the sound.

Around the next turn, a man stood over a woman who was rocking back and forth on the ground.

The cowboy ducked behind a tree almost at the same time as Leah. She noted his familiarity with law enforcement tactics.

"Get your hands in the air where I can see them and stay right where you are," Leah commanded.

The man, who wore a hoodie, took a couple of steps back and thrust his hands in the air.

"Freeze," Leah said. She appreciated Deacon not going rogue and trying to take over the situation. Some people would. She kept one eye on Hoodie while she asked the woman, "Where are you hurt?"

"My leg. I tripped over something," the woman managed to shout in bursts through forced breaths. "Didn't see those rocks and rolled my ankle."

"I'm going to get you some help. First, I need a little more information." She could see the woman was in agony. One of the first rules of good policing was never run to an injured party. The man standing over her could use the move to his advantage and attack. Or, this could be a setup to throw her off base where she could be ambushed. There could be others waiting to jump out from the nearby brush. Leah had been trained not to take the chance. Given that she had a three-year-old son who'd be orphaned if anything happened to her, she doubled down on cautious police work. Her primary goal at the beginning of every shift—like most officers she knew—was to make it home to loved ones safely.

"*You*, sit down and keep your hands where I can see them," Leah demanded of the man.

He dropped down.

Leah wasn't quite ready to holster her gun. "What's your name, ma'am?"

"Stacy Rutledge." She was rocking back and forth faster.

"Mind if I check on her?" Deacon asked.

"Go ahead," Leah stated.

"*You* with the hoodie. What's your name?" she asked the man sitting back on his heels with his hands folded around the back of his neck.

"Kevin Lee," the man said.

For all she knew, Kevin wasn't really his name. He might've intended to take advantage of a woman who'd been injured on her run. Of course, he didn't have to be the murderer from last night in order to be a criminal. There were plenty of other types of crimes against women.

Her imagination was running wild, getting the best of her on this one and she knew it.

She thought about the fact that there'd been no witnesses to the crime last night, no description of the perp.

Tonight's run had been a bad idea from the start.

No matter how hard she'd tried, she couldn't shake the feeling of being watched.

"Show me your face," Leah demanded.

"I need to move my hands to do that." Kevin sounded scared and confused. His reaction said he was caught off guard and most likely didn't have criminal intent.

"Only enough to remove your hoodie," she stated with authority.

He complied, revealing short black hair. He had a prominent nose set on an otherwise average clean-cut face. No warning bells sounded based on his looks but she had no description of the man from last night's deadly attack to work with and no criminal profile yet. Whoever had attacked Jillian Mitchell had been strong enough to drag her off the trail, subdue her and then sever her right ankle. Her body had been carried deeper into the brush. Dirt underneath her fingernails indicated she'd put up a good fight. There were other signs, bruises on her body.

Maybe the investigator would get lucky and get a DNA hit.

It was presumed the suspect had worn gloves.

Investigators were still trying to determine if Jillian was murdered by someone she knew—which was the most likely case for a female—or if the attack had been random. Someone close to her would know her evening routine. The person had to be strong enough to subdue Jillian, drag her off the trail and carry her through the trees based on the fact that there were no signs of her being dragged there. Leah was certain she'd seen the woman before. The same people came out night after night. She'd found the same to be true in the mornings, too. After her rookie year she'd been placed on the deep night shift. The excitement and stress of the job caused her to start jogging in order to wind down enough to sleep during the day. Her clock had been turned upside down in those years. The routine comforted her.

"What are you doing here, Kevin?" An obvious question but one that had to be asked.

"Jogging." His voice was incredulous.

Of course, everyone feared a serial killer in the making but a next-day attack would have been unlikely in this scenario. Seasoned serial killers took time to bake.

The lead investigator happened to be her ex

and although she'd believed the split was amicable—it had been a long time coming—Charles Dougherty had been short with her ever since. Six months had passed now. With his attitude, she was beginning to question whether or not he'd agreed with her assessment or if he'd been playing along so she wouldn't realize how much the breakup actually had hurt.

She'd overheard a fellow officer refer to her as Cold-Fish Cordon when she'd walked past the men's locker room. Charles had laughed, not defended her.

And that was just the beginning of the cold-shoulder treatment she'd been getting from him ever since.

"Any other reason you're out here tonight, Kevin?" she asked.

"Other than my nightly run? No," he said with a quizzical look.

A good investigator asked every question, and especially the ones she thought she knew the answers to. Because every once in a while a witness answered wrong and gave her the leverage she needed to keep digging.

Chapter Three

Kevin Lee was innocent. All Leah had needed was five minutes to assess his guilt or innocence. Her years of experience had honed her instincts. As much as she trusted them, she never took them for granted. But the man was as clean as Sunday's sheets on a freshly made bed.

An officer had arrived, followed shortly after by paramedics. The scene bustled with activity. Between the detour with Deacon Kent and the injured jogger, it was getting late. Leah checked her watch. She should've been home fifteen minutes ago to relieve her sitter. Normally, that wouldn't have been a problem but tensions were running high.

"Excuse me, I need to make a phone call," she said to Deacon.

"Someone expecting you at home?" he asked. An emotion flickered behind his gray-blue eyes that she couldn't quite pinpoint.

"Sort of," she admitted for reasons she had

yet to pick apart. The question had caught her off guard. She walked out of earshot in order to make the call to her babysitter.

Riley answered on the first ring. The soft hum of the TV that was on in the background comforted Leah.

"Everything okay?" Riley immediately asked. Her next-door neighbor was great about coming over after Connor had gone to sleep so that Leah could get in her run. Leah would miss that next fall when Riley left for college.

"I'm giving a statement to police right now about a jogger being hurt on the trail," Leah informed her.

"Another one?" Riley's tone was ominous. Her voice dropped as she asked, "Are you okay?"

"This was an accident. It's not related," Leah said quickly. Too quickly.

"Oh." Riley must've picked up on it. Everyone's nerves were on edge following the attack.

"How's Connor?" Leah wanted an update on her son but she also wanted to redirect Riley.

"Hasn't budged an inch since I got here," Riley reported. "In fact, he hasn't made a peep but I checked on him fifteen minutes ago, anyway."

"His preschool teacher said they spent a lot of time outdoors today and that the class should sleep well tonight." Leah couldn't remember what a good night's sleep was anymore. To sleep like an innocent child again. What would that be like?

Either way, Leah was grateful for her high school neighbor, who was close to the back half of her senior year. Riley's job was basically to make sure Connor didn't wake or need anything. The high schooler brought her laptop computer and Leah figured had knocked out most of her college applications while sitting on her couch. It was mutually beneficial because Riley complained about her brothers, twins, who were star football players on the middle school team. She said there wasn't a safe place in the house with those two running, shouting and throwing the ball just about everywhere. There were always a few of their friends on hand, and since Riley's room was directly across the hall from the twins', she couldn't get a minute of peace.

Since Leah offered money, going to her house was certainly cheaper than going to a coffeehouse and dropping five bucks on a latte every time she wanted to use the free Wi-Fi.

The arrangement worked out well for both of them. Since Leah didn't get off work until six o'clock most nights, she barely had a pair of hours to spend with Connor before his bedtime. Rather than sit inside the house and stare at four walls after he was tucked into bed, Leah had made the proposition to Riley a year ago and the arrangement seemed to be working out for them both.

"I should be home soon," Leah promised.

"Take your time. Seriously. I have nowhere else to go but home." Leah almost smiled because she could practically hear Riley rolling her eyes.

Leah couldn't feel guilty about being later than usual with an attitude like that. Her place was a refuge for Riley and Leah didn't mind helping out the girl. Riley seemed to think it was cute that strangers thought they were sisters and had mentioned more than once that she wished it were true.

"I won't be too late," Leah promised. She wasn't ready to leave the scene just yet. She needed to remind the handsome rancher that he had no business digging around a crime scene and that he could end up a suspect if he refused to listen to her.

She figured that would go over about as well as whipped cream on a taco.

"TELL ME MORE about the case," Deacon said to the detective once the jogger had been carried away by the paramedics, Kevin Lee's statement had been given and the scene had quieted down.

The detective shot him a look that left no

question as to what she thought about his request. "I can't."

"I'm not telling you to give away your family's barbecue recipe. I'd like to know who I'm looking for, if you have a description of the suspect. It'll help us on the ranch as we guard our herd and we might actually be of some help if he returns," Deacon said. He could ask the same information from his cousin Zach, but the detective might have an inside track.

"We don't have one," she admitted. "And I'm not the lead on this case, so I have no authority whatsoever to dig deeper. All we're doing that I know of is watching the trail and pretty much everywhere else for another attack."

"There were no witnesses and you have no leads," he summarized.

"Just like the newspaper said," she stated.

"Excuse me if I don't believe everything I read," he countered.

"Your cousin. He's the sheriff, right?" she asked.

"Yes." Deacon wasn't sure where she was going with this.

"Explains why you know how to conduct yourself during an investigation." She locked on to his gaze and he ignored the power that one look held. He also saw a repeat of that split-second vulnerability that got all his protective instincts fired up. A glance at her finger had said she didn't wear a wedding band. But that call home had thrown him off balance at first until he heard bits and pieces of her conversation. "Also tells me that you won't mind me reminding you that I'm not privileged to share information with you. Even if I had access to it, which I don't."

There were ways to get around that but he didn't want to push her.

"Want to grab a cup of coffee?" he asked, noticing she'd started shivering. The temperature had dropped another ten degrees. He could feel it through his jacket. Christmas was around the corner, so there was no shock that the weather had turned.

"No, thank you." Her words were curt. "But I will share another piece of advice if you don't mind."

"Be my guest." He folded his arms across his chest.

"If you go crawling around a crime scene, you might just leave *your* DNA for someone to discover and end up on the wrong side here. Why not leave this to law enforcement."

"My cousin has no authority in Fort Worth. I have no idea if these cases are connected but have every intention of finding out before any more of my cattle suffer and heaven forbid another person if that's what's happening here. I'll give you that I acted on impulse coming here. Doesn't mean I regret my actions and especially not if I can help in any way." Getting away from the ranch for a few hours had proven to be the distraction he needed. While his brothers seemed to have settled into their birthright, Deacon still wasn't comfortable. He'd been restless since losing his parents and leaving his small but thriving Dallas-based custom millwork company. He'd sold the business to his partner not without regret.

Leah examined him and he noticed that her eyes darkened when she skimmed his torso.

"Maybe you shouldn't act on impulse next time." She pointed her finger at his chest.

"What are you not telling me?" The detective was holding back. He couldn't say he was surprised given the circumstances. The statement caught her off guard enough for him to know he'd hit the nail on the head.

Leah's cell buzzed. She checked the screen and Deacon caught the breath she blew out.

"Cordon here," she said into the phone and he realized the caller couldn't be the sitter who waited for her at home. The stab of jealousy said he feared it was a romantic interest. She turned around to face the opposite direction to take the call.

"That's great news, sir," she said quietly.

"Thank you," she added before ending the call and turning around to face Deacon.

"That wasn't home calling," he said matter-of-factly.

"Nope," she reported. "Killer's been arrested. We can all go home."

LEAH STARED AT her bedroom ceiling. A light streamed in from the window, enabling her to see clearly. A cursory glance at the clock said the sun wouldn't be up for three hours. A pair of hours after that and Connor would be awake and ready to go full tilt, as only three-year-olds knew how to do. So why was she still awake, thinking about the Porter's Bend Killer, when she should have been deep in REM sleep by now?

The killer was in jail. Details of his murder would be out soon enough. Maybe she could go in to work early and stop off at the coroner's office on the way in. Connor's preschool opened at 6:00 a.m. and she'd had to take advantage of the extra hours for cases from time to time. The director, Mrs. Clark, wouldn't be shocked if Leah showed up with Connor on short notice. The arrangement at Marymount Day School had worked well so far.

Another urge struck.

The impulse to call Deacon Kent and discuss the case was strong.

An unsettled feeling crept over her. If this case was wrapped up, why was she wide-awake in the middle of the night, staring at the rain spot on the ceiling? The perp behind bars had a rap sheet long enough to make his arrest feasible.

Leah reminded herself that this case was too close to home. She was losing her objectivity. A murder had occurred on her jogging path, the trail she took every night before bed in order to clear her head. She bit back the irony that she was a detective and couldn't keep her own trail safe.

How many times had Leah and Jillian Mitchell possibly looked up and nodded while passing each other without really giving each other much thought? Dozens? More?

No good could come out of digging around in her ex's case. Leah should have been able to let this go and walk away, sleep easy. And she would do just that.

She would close the book on this one as soon as she called Deacon Kent.

Chapter Four

Deacon rolled onto his side and stared at the clock. It read 3:43 a.m. Most of his family would be up in the next half hour, as well as his cousin Zach, the Broward County Sheriff.

The same couple of questions recycled. Could the trail murderer be the same man they'd been looking for in Jacobstown? Most people by now believed that the man responsible for the brutal killings of half a dozen heifers and even more small animals in various ranches across the state would move on to human targets. It made even more sense that the man would go after a woman, considering all the animal deaths reported so far had been females.

Folks in Jacobstown were jumpy and rightfully so. People started locking their doors, an act so foreign it seemed strange even to him to have to think about. People who used to leave cars running when they ran inside the post office to pick up mail from a PO box had changed habits. Everyone had buttoned up in the wake of the incidents.

Anyone new was suspect now instead of welcomed like in the past. The town had a long tradition of being family friendly but times had changed. People had changed. And fear—a foreign emotion—gripped the townsfolk.

Deacon thought about the detective from earlier. She'd put up a brave front but he'd seen the panic in her eyes. Leah Cordon lingering in his mind was as productive as pouring milk over asparagus.

Deacon sat up, rubbed his eyes and threw his feet over the side of the bed. Since sleep was out of the question, he might as well get up and do something industrious. His brothers and the ranch hands would be awake soon and he wanted to deliver the news personally that the Fort Worth Police had arrested the person responsible for the attack at Porter's Bend. If there was any possible link between this guy and the person responsible for butchering animals on the family land, everyone would want to know about it.

Deacon's thoughts again wandered into territory he knew better than to go—Leah Cordon.

He'd moved into his bungalow-style house on the ranch six months ago, the day after it had finished being built. Living here was convenient and he appreciated having his own space. He'd always been that kid who kept to the sidelines and did his own thing. Not much had changed since becoming a man. He'd probably laugh if someone described him as the strong, silent type but he couldn't argue.

Having his own place gave him breathing room, even though he didn't feel like he fit the rancher's life. His older brother, Mitch, had taken to it like a fisherman to a pond. The baby of the family, Amber, followed in their eldest brother's footsteps. But he and his three other brothers, Will, Nate and Jordan, fell somewhere in the cracks. Don't get him wrong, he loved Texas and the family business. Being out on the range and sleeping under the stars kept him sane. It was the rest—the part where his entire life was planned out before him—that made his collar feel like a noose.

The ringtone of his cell caught him off guard. He hopped into his jeans and got to his phone that was vibrating on his dresser.

Leah Cordon's name was on the screen.

"What's up, Detective?" Deacon asked.

"Sorry to wake you." She sounded like she'd had a shot of espresso.

"I haven't slept." Deacon sat on the edge of the chair next to his dresser, thinking he wouldn't mind a cup of black coffee. He raked his free hand through his hair.

"What's keeping you awake?" Her voice had a sexy ring to it, a campfire-and-moonlight-under-the-stars quality. And that was something he had no place noticing given the nature of their friendship—a word he'd use lightly to describe their liaison.

"Most likely the same reason your eyes are still open." The line went quiet for a second and he wondered if she were debating whether or not it had been a good idea to call him.

"I'm heading over to the coroner's office in a little while to see the body," she finally said. "Something feels off."

"What do you think you'll find there?" His curiosity was piqued.

"Not sure yet," she admitted.

"But you think it's worth it to make the drive over." He was stating the obvious but it didn't hurt to make sure they were on the same page. He'd learned a long time ago not to assume he knew what anyone else was thinking.

She agreed that she did. Another few beats of silence permeated the line. Then came, "Your heifers. They suffered, didn't they?"

"Yes." He let his tone reflect his frustration.

"You mentioned smaller animals, too," she continued.

"There've been rabbits." He switched hands with the phone and put it to his left ear.

"No weapons were ever recovered." It was a statement of fact, not a question.

"And no DNA was left behind," he added. "What are you getting at?"

"In your best guess, what kind of weapon was used?" Her voice had a quiet calm and he assumed it was the one she used to get people to confide in her. He would've anyway because he didn't have anything to hide.

"A jigsaw," he said.

The line was dead quiet for several beats and he could tell the wheels in her mind were spinning. "I thought that's what I read. This guy made a clean cut." She paused a few more beats before adding, "I'm sorry about your animals."

"Are you still going to the coroner's office?" he asked.

"I am," she confirmed.

"Mind if I show up? I'd like to get a look for myself and your badge will get me through the door." He could get to Fort Worth in about an hour. Judging her reactions so far, she didn't believe the man sitting in jail had committed the crime.

"I have no authority in this investigation," she said quietly. The killer had murdered someone on her trail. Based on the description of Jillian Mitchell, the two looked similar. Did the detective think it could've easily been her, instead?

He understood when a crime hit a little too close to home. He knew the fear that could instill in people.

"I might be able to help with that." With Deacon's family name he could probably call in a few favors and get a private visit with the body of the victim without rattling too many cages. But he hoped the detective would take him with her. All she had to do was flash her badge and he wouldn't have to have his name tied to the investigation.

"You know what, I made a mistake calling. Forget what I said. I'm sorry to bother you. I should go." What had happened in the last few seconds to change her mind? Was it the fact that he'd used the Kent last name? That normally opened doors instead of closing them. Of course, she might not want to be associated with anyone who was high profile. That could draw attention to her.

"Hold on a minute, I—"

It was too late. The line went dead.

LEAH PULLED INTO the parking lot of the Tarrant County Coroner's office. Dr. Timothy Rex had been with the city since long before her time and he was one of the most respected people she had the privilege of working with.

She'd no sooner put the gearshift in Park than

movement on the east side of the parking lot caught her eye. A pickup truck door opened and Deacon Kent got out of the driver's side. Her stomach gave a little flip at seeing Deacon Kent again. She ignored her reaction to him, even though instinctively she checked her face in the mirror. She should've known he would show. She'd all but invited him on the phone, and had regretted it almost instantly. It wasn't like her to act on impulse, which is exactly what she'd done when she'd picked up her cell at almost four o'clock in the morning.

Speaking of which, lack of sleep had dark circles cradling her eyes. She'd never been one to do well without sleep, even though she'd gotten very little of it during her high school years. Unlike her peers, she wasn't lying awake at night, staring at the ceiling because she worried she'd fail a test. Her stress levels reached far deeper than that. While everyone else met up on Friday nights to find out who would host the next party after *Friday Night Lights*, she churned all night feeling physically ill. She thought about what she could've done differently. Her mind stirred on how she'd let her friend down in the worst possible way.

Leah pushed those heavy thoughts aside and stepped out of her car. She didn't bother asking what he was doing there.

"Good morning, Mr. Kent." He was already making a beeline toward her by the time she climbed out of her driver's seat.

"Call me Deacon," he said. "I hope it's okay that I'm here."

"You have a vested interest in this case and so do I." She left out the part where she liked having someone to bounce ideas off of for a change. For too long it had just been her and her three-year-old son, Connor. Even when she'd dated Detective Dougherty, she hadn't felt the sense of—what?—comfort that she instantly felt with Deacon. She chalked it up to it being easier to talk to a stranger than those closest at times. But nothing felt strange about Deacon Kent. In a way, she felt like she'd known him for years and it was probably just because he was easy to talk to. She didn't want to get inside her head about what that meant, so she just let it be.

There were four cars parked in the lot at this early hour aside from Deacon's truck and her sedan. It wouldn't be difficult to see if anyone came in or out.

"The Mitchell case isn't mine to ask questions about. So I have a Jane Doe who came in three nights ago that we'll say you might be able to ID. According to witnesses, she's a vagrant and you won't recognize her but that's not the point—"

"You're looking for an excuse to walk in the door," he finished the sentence for her.

"That's right."

Leah badged them inside the building and then led Deacon down a hospital-like white-tiled hallway that led to a glass door. Etched on it were the words *Dr. Timothy Rex* along with a series of alphabet letters to indicate his degrees.

At sixty-eight, Dr. Rex, aka T-Rex was still a crackerjack. His mind was sharper than most thirty-year-olds she knew, which wasn't exactly an endorsement for the people in her circle. Leah almost laughed out loud. Her circle consisted of the people she knew at work, her babysitter and a three-year-old. Unless she counted the purple dinosaur from Allen, Texas, whose voice she could hear in her sleep thanks to Connor binge-watching the DVDs. Did they call it binge-watching when it was almost-constant background noise and some of the same episodes over and over again?

Leah made a move for the metal bar to open the door but Deacon beat her to it. She couldn't remember the last time a man had opened a door for her. She was independent and strong. She didn't need a man to open doors. But there was something sweet and chivalrous about the gesture that caused her stomach to do another round of somersaults.

Old-fashioned chivalry was still a turn-on. She mumbled a thank-you and caught a small smile toying with the corner of his lips—lips she had no business focusing on.

There was no receptionist working this early. Leah had expected that. She didn't have credentials to badge through the next set of doors leading to the lab. Dr. Rex looked up at her. He rocked his head as though he'd been expecting her. He hadn't. She'd given him no warning. His manner had always been welcoming. That was just Rex.

He hurried over to the door, first removing his examination gloves and tossing them into the wastepaper basket positioned next to the door. He acknowledged Deacon with another smile after letting them in.

Deacon stuck out his hand as the door closed behind him.

T-Rex took it with a vigorous shake, introducing himself. His eyes sparked for the briefest moment when he heard Deacon's last name. She figured that happened a lot, even though nothing about the down-to-earth cowboy screamed that he was one of the wealthiest men in Texas. Leah almost couldn't wrap her mind around it. She came from money. Or, more accurately, her parents had money. They still did because she refused to let their money manipulate her and that's exactly what they'd tried to use it for. As an only child, she blamed being the sole focus of their manipulation efforts on the lack of siblings to spread the "wealth" of their attention across.

Leah had gone to the police academy after getting her degree in criminal justice. Neither her philosophy-professor father nor her board-of-directors mother approved of her degree and that's the reason they'd stated when they refused to pay tuition for her to go to the out-of-state college she wanted to attend. So she'd played the child-of-a-professor card and went to the University of Texas at Arlington instead. Being the child of faculty gave her free tuition and that had helped not to rack up education expenses. Now she couldn't imagine trying to bring up a child on a detective's salary and repay college loans.

T-Rex was given his nickname for his turtle-like shoulders and arms. It might've been cruel except that he'd been the one to make the joke and the name stuck. He said he'd had it since college and didn't mind. T-Rex, after all, had been an apex predator. The real story behind it was that he'd broken both of his arms as a child. His missionary parents who traveled with him abroad had made sure he'd received the best available care. But he'd been given medical attention in a developing country. The incident had left him unable to lift his arms over his head. He liked to say he got a PhD and an MD because he couldn't get the alphabet letters from his boyhood aspiration, NFL.

Otherwise, he was tall-ish. Admittedly, standing next to Deacon Kent made T-Rex look smaller. His spectacles slid down on his nose—much like pictures of Santa Claus. With the resemblance, there were other monikers T-Rex could've picked up. He had the same belly and carriage as the guy who made midnight rounds one night a year, a night that was coming soon. T-Rex also had a slow smile and quick wit. Both were genuine.

"How's the grandbaby?" Leah always asked about the five-year-old light of his life, Harley. She'd come to live with him and his wife after losing his daughter to a rare bone disease. The father had never been in the picture.

"Growing like a weed." He beamed. It couldn't be easy to take on a child at his and his wife's age. But he was the kind of man who wouldn't turn his back on someone who needed him and especially not family. "She decided she needs to learn how to do a cartwheel."

"What does she need to do that for?" Leah asked with a little more enthusiasm than she felt. She *did* care. Don't get her wrong. But she was biding her time until she could ask what she wanted, what was on the tip of her tongue.

T-Rex rolled his eyes. "She's made up a list of all the things she needs to do while she's still *young*."

"She still thinking kindergarten is the end of her childhood?" Leah couldn't help but smile. The kid was a cutup and Leah figured she got half her personality from her grandfather. If she got half of his big heart, she'd do fine in life.

He nodded before turning his attention to Deacon. "You got kids?"

"Me? No." Deacon's response was a little too quick.

Leah almost asked what he had against kids. She figured it was none of her business what he thought about anything, except that a little piece of her argued that she did care. And more than she wanted to acknowledge to herself.

T-Rex must've picked up on her tension because he redirected his focus. "What brings you to my humble abode so early in the morning?"

"I need to see Jane Doe," she said.

"Ah." T-Rex's gaze bounced from her to Deacon.

"His friend is missing and she fits my Jane Doe's description." Leah didn't like being dishonest. But if she inserted herself into Charles

Dougherty's investigation and asked the questions she wanted to outright ask, Charles could make her life at work even harder than he had been.

"Right this way."

Chapter Five

T-Rex motioned toward another hallway that led to another freezing cold room that had been dubbed The Meat Locker by beat cops.

Leah thought the term was disrespectful and had been teased her rookie year for not embracing the lingo. She also thought about her high school friend being inside a place like that and an icy chill trickled down her spine. She thought about the fact that Millie's—short for Mildred, which was her aunt's name—parents would have been brought down to a place like this in order to ID their daughter's body, a fate no parent should ever have to face.

"Heard you got a new one in night before. The Mitchell case." Leah figured there'd been enough casual conversation between the three of them this morning that she could start peppering in her questions. She also knew in her gut—from years of honing investigative skills—that T-Rex's guard was down.

"Phone's been ringing off the hook ever since. I unplugged it." The case was big-time and people would be interested. He wouldn't think anything of a few random-sounding questions.

"Mayor's office?" she asked casually.

T-Rex nodded. He paused in front of The Meat Locker. "Sad case."

"Heard her foot was missing," she said.

"Cut clean off. One slice." He turned to look them in the eyes. He always did that when he was delivering news that most people would consider disturbing. Leah had learned to keep an emotional distance from cases. That, and her nightly run were the only reasons she could sleep at all and still be able to do the kind of work she did. She gave families peace of mind. She couldn't bring a loved one back, but knowing what had happened built a bridge to healing. Without it, becoming whole again would always be on the opposite shore, out of reach.

Deacon, who had been quiet up until now, folded his arms. Strong, silent type? He seemed to take everything in. See what most people couldn't because they were too busy talking, trying to get a point across.

"Any idea what he used?" she asked T-Rex.

"Hatchet, maybe." T-Rex shook his head. "She was young. Whole life ahead of her."

She liked that he thought of the people who

landed on his table in terms of being real human beings. People with parents, spouses, children. She'd heard stories of other coroners who'd mentally detached to the point they thought of people as projects.

"It's awful." Leah could only hope her friend Millie had been taken to someone as caring.

"She fought back, though," he stated.

"Good for her." Leah knew she would. There was no way she'd ever go down easy if faced with a similar situation. She'd take out an eye or anything else she could of her attacker. For one, she wouldn't stop trying to break free until she took her last breath. Secondly, she knew that she'd leave behind valuable DNA evidence if she clawed and kicked.

Millie had willingly gone with her abductor. With what Leah knew now, she realized she and Millie had probably known the person who'd taken her. He was most likely someone they trusted.

"I heard her ankle was cut clean. That true?" Leah asked.

"Yes." T-Rex led them inside the frigid room. The wall with drawers still made her queasy as she walked toward it but she swallowed the bile rising in her throat.

He stopped at the last one on the right, bottom drawer. He pulled out a long table. Deacon watched as the body bag was unzipped and then the face of a woman who looked frozen in time, Jane Doe, was revealed. She was found on a playground swing after a pair of nights with temperatures in the teens. At first blush, it looked like she'd frozen to death until Leah walked around behind the body and saw a bullet hole.

He shook his head. "It's not her."

T-Rex attended to sealing up as Leah thanked him for his time. Deacon followed her outside, still saying very little. In the parking lot, Leah paused at her sedan. Deacon had slipped on sunglasses from his jacket pocket and between those and his Stetson his eyes were hooded.

"There a place we can grab a cup of coffee?" he asked.

She needed to pick his brain about the heifers for a few minutes before he disappeared out of her life. "There's a little place around the corner."

"I'll follow you." She ignored the deep rumble rippling through his voice. Any other circumstances and she'd want to get to know Deacon Kent better on a personal level. She knew deep down she'd never allow herself to get close to a man like him. There was something different about him, something she couldn't quite pinpoint but felt like a threat. Maybe it was the fact he was the kind of person she could fall for. Being near him brought out feelings she'd thought long since dead. Besides, she had Connor to think about, and after dating Charles Dougherty, the last thing she needed to do was complicate her life further. She'd done a bang-up job with the last one.

Leah hopped into her sedan and led the way to Marvin's Diner. It was one of those eateries that looked like a silver bullet train on the outside, complete with red vinyl benches and '70s throwback decor on the inside.

She parked away from the front door where there were two parking spots together in the almost full lot. Marvin's was always bristling with activity at this time and kept hours from 5:00 a.m. to 3:00 p.m. Breakfast and lunch were all that was on the menu. Ask any cop what he or she had in common with New York City cabdrivers and he or she would say both always knew the best places to eat.

Leah got out of her car and waited for Deacon. Again, her heart thudded against her rib cage when she saw him. He'd taken off his sunglasses and hat, leaving them inside his pickup. Rays of sunlight streaked his hair. His eyes were steel gray.

Detective Andrew McKeever, aka Keeve, came walking out the door to Marvin's as Deacon made a move for the handle.

"Hello, Keeve." Leah felt compelled to greet the man. He was one of Charles's closest friends—which wasn't saying a lot since Charles had pushed nearly everyone out of his life—and had been cold-shouldering Leah ever since the breakup. Keeve needed to get over it and she figured she'd kill him with kindness because the two of them had always had a solid professional relationship. Years ago, marrying Connor's father, a detective, had made her think it would be okay to see someone socially from work. She quickly realized after Charles the flaws in that thinking. Because she and Wyatt Cordon had had a beautiful child together, whereas she and Charles had had a fling that ended badly, leaving a whole bunch of messiness in its wake.

Keeve's gaze bounced from her to Deacon and back. His face muscles tensed. "Detective."

That one word had such a dismissive quality in it that Leah didn't bother to respond.

Keeve walked right past her, his gaze locking on to Deacon whose face of hard angles and planes gave away nothing of his reaction.

As they headed inside, Sunny Bowman, the diner's most popular waitress, grabbed two menus. "How many in your party, hon?"

"The two of us," Deacon responded.

She smiled at him and her cheeks flamed. Leah could only hope her own reaction to seeing Deacon for the first time wasn't so obvious. A stab of jealousy she had no right to own caught her off guard.

"Right this way, Detective," Sunny said. She was midthirties but looked older when Leah focused on the lines etched in the woman's face. Her poufy white hair was in pigtails and her lashes were so long they practically touched her eyebrows. Sunny worked her hips when she walked and good food wasn't the only reason so many male officers hung out at the diner.

Sunny stopped at a booth in the far corner, Leah's favorite, and spun around with her arm out like she was presenting a new car to a game show winner.

"Thanks, Sunny," Leah said. Before today, Sunny's flirtatious personality hadn't felt like fingernails on a chalkboard.

To Deacon's credit, he didn't seem to notice. Was it his good upbringing that made him such a gentleman? She'd read about his family. The Kents seemed like the best of the best, unlike her family, which was all surface and no substance. Her parents had tried to persuade her to at least become an attorney if she insisted on going down the path of criminal justice. When she'd told them she wanted to be a cop and then a homicide detective, they'd gone down a familiar road, reminding her she couldn't bring her friend back by putting herself in danger. She'd have liked to believe they were worried about her safety, but then she'd heard her mother on the phone with Leah's aunt, talking about how embarrassing it was that Leah didn't have more ambition. That she'd always be stuck feeling sorry for herself for losing her best friend. Her mother had no idea then and nothing had improved since.

"Did you want coffee, Detective?" Sunny blinked at Leah expectantly.

"Yes. Thank you." Leah must've zoned out there for a second.

"And for you?" Sunny's smile widened when she looked at Deacon, who didn't look up from the menu.

"I would, thanks."

"Cream and sugar?" she asked.

"Black."

"Same for me," Leah said, unable to suppress a satisfied smirk. Based on the look on Sunny's face, she wasn't used to being anything other than the center of attention from male patrons.

It was probably just the smart girl in her that wanted to prove brains could be beautiful. She'd been gawky and awkward in high school and losing her friend made her want to disappear even more. Leah's mother used to tell her that she could've been beautiful if she'd put in the effort. Even a successful businesswoman could prize looks over substance, Leah had realized.

Wow, what had her examining her past like this out of the blue? There was something about the Jillian Mitchell case that hit too close to home.

Leah pretended to focus on the menu but she was really lost in her own thoughts, ever aware of the strong male presence sitting across from her. She was surprised to find him staring at her when she looked up.

"Everything's good here. It's all farm to table," she said, trying to detract attention away from the blush crawling up her neck.

"Wrong foot. Wrong MO," he suddenly said to her.

Chapter Six

Sunny walked up with two cups of coffee. She bent closer to Deacon, showing her considerable cleavage and Leah was certain she heard a harrumph sound when Deacon had no reaction.

Leah picked up her cup and took a swig, the hot coffee a welcome burn on her throat. She needed a clear head if she was going to make progress on the investigation and keep her thoughts from wandering into unwelcomed territory when it came to Deacon.

As soon as Sunny took their orders and disappeared, Deacon's gaze settled on Leah.

"You picked up on that." She referred to the wrong foot. It was easy to see that a different MO had been used.

He nodded and then sipped his coffee. "The scenario at our ranches doesn't fit the Porter's Bend Killer. But a man's in jail."

"Eyewitness places him in the park. He has a violent past," she said.

"Was a murder weapon recovered?" he asked.

"Nope."

"Then it's a flimsy case at best," he said. "They won't be able to hold the guy for long."

"His background is an issue for him." She ran her finger along the rim of her coffee mug.

"Meaning?" The statement got Deacon's attention.

"His crimes against women have been escalating. He has a decent-sized rap sheet." She picked up the cup, rolling it in her palms for the warmth.

"But chopping off someone's foot seems harsh for someone who is escalating their violence," he stated.

"This case reads like a revenge killing to me. It's violent and personal." Her body shivered involuntarily, thinking about what had happened to Jillian Mitchell.

"But why the foot?" Deacon's brows crinkled in concentration. She didn't want to think of the move as adorable. It helped that his face muscles tensed. It seemed to dawn on him. "The killer wants to send police on a wild-goose chase."

"A copycat who cut off a foot…" Leah didn't finish her thought before she saw Charles walk into the restaurant out of the corner of her eye. Had Keeve alerted Charles to the fact that she was here? *Son of a—*

Charles Dougherty made a beeline for her

table. His gaze zeroed in on Deacon. Looking at her ex now, she couldn't see what she'd ever seen in him. Friendship? Kinship? Comfort? Familiarity? Charles had been a sympathetic ear after being alone for two and a half years following the loss of Wyatt, a man she'd truly cared about. Raising a child on her own had been tough and she wasn't making excuses, but after Charles lost his teenage daughter to a rare childhood cancer and then his wife walked out, Leah had felt for the guy.

She'd needed a friend when Wyatt had died but she'd been pregnant and alone. Her only other friend at work, Susan, had a family of her own. Leah's parents had all but disowned her after she'd refused to *take care* of the situation. She'd quickly told them that her baby wasn't a *situation*. That had gone over about as well as the day she'd come home and declared her college major.

She had been faced with bringing up a child alone with no support from her parents and no other family to speak of, since Wyatt had been brought up by grandparents who were long since dead. Wyatt had been twenty years her senior and she'd overheard her mother's accusation that Leah had *daddy issues* days before she'd married him. Her parents hadn't been fans of her husband, her marriage or her child. Connor was innocent in all this and it burned her up to think they could turn their backs on their only grandchild.

Deacon turned, seeming to catch on to the heat being thrown off by Charles's glare. Charles made quick strides to the table and then stopped. Deacon didn't take his eyes off Charles but stood to greet him. Leah figured it was primal on his part because no one would stay sitting when a charging bull was coming toward him.

Charles took a step back as he looked up at Deacon, who stuck his hand out and introduced himself. Deacon Kent could keep a calm head under pressure. Another thing she liked about him. The list of his good qualities was growing longer.

"Detective," Charles said to her.

"What can we do for you?" Leah noticed that Charles's previously puffed-out chest had deflated once he got a good look at Deacon. Deacon had a solid six inches in height on him, with a broad chest and stacked muscles.

At five feet ten, Charles was one of the taller cops in the department. Most of her colleagues were a few inches shorter and beat cops even more so. Charles's expression was still cocky, like he acknowledged that Deacon Kent had him in size but that Charles's weapon evened the score a little bit. It didn't.

"Outside, Detective," Charles barked, looking past Deacon, who moved to put his heft in between her and her ex.

Deacon was smart enough to pick up on the tension radiating off Charles. The rancher had to know more was up between them than work.

"Anything you have to say can be said inside the restaurant, Charles," she said calmly. No reason to bait a bull. Charles was in a huff about something and she wondered how many of his buddies were watching her. The relationship between Leah and Charles had been over for a long time.

Charles's lips thinned and his gaze narrowed. He might not like her response but she wasn't going outside with him.

"Then take a walk with me." His tone softened but his gaze hardened.

"I'm having a cup of coffee. I'm fine sitting right here," she said.

Charles took a threatening step toward her. Deacon put his hand on Charles's shoulder to stop him.

"What do you say we head outside and talk man-to-man?" Deacon's voice was a study in calm. No matter how menacing Charles's demeanor had become, Deacon didn't seem threatened in the least by it. That kind of confidence was yet another thing to add to the growing list of qualities Leah liked in Deacon. Once, she and Charles had been in a restaurant and another couple had been seated before them. Granted, it was a mistake on the hostess's part. But Charles's reaction had been over the top. Leah immediately wondered what he would have done if Connor misbehaved in front of him. Charles didn't have patience and that was one of the many reasons the two were never introduced.

Connor was an amazing kid. He was a good kid. But he was a kid. He had his moments.

If Charles couldn't have patience with a hostess who was doing her best, how on earth would he handle the trials of a kid? His attitude had developed later, and he clearly wasn't dealing with his emotions from losing a child. That's the way Leah viewed potential mates now. How would they handle Connor? Because a great kid deserved to have amazing men in his life.

"I don't have any business with you," Charles fired back.

"Anything you have to say to me can be said in front of my friend," Leah said.

"Fine." Charles crossed his arms over his chest and placed his feet a few feet apart in an athletic stance. He had an athletic build. He was mostly arms and chest. He was neither overly good-looking nor overly bad looking. He had brown hair and almost black eyes with a slightly bulbous nose, which was pug-like. His skin was tan and clear, and a lot of the women at the station perked up when he entered a room, their voices a flirtier pitch. He dressed more like he was on SWAT than as a detective. Not being able to use his size to intimidate Deacon Kent must have been very frustrating. Charles had a sharp wit and a sharper tongue. If there truly were a good cop/bad cop routine, Charles would have been the bad cop. Had that been the initial pull? He was good-looking by most standards and came off as emotionally detached. He wasn't, though. In fact, she'd quickly realized that underneath the layers of bulldog exterior he was insecure. That was the reason he yelled at hostesses who made innocent mistakes. His tactic worked with some types of people in investigations. It just wasn't the tact she took with people if she could avoid it. Her touch was lighter and she figured she got more information out of people that way. What was that old saying about catching more flies with honey? She was honey. Charles was fire.

"What were you doing at the morgue earlier?" Charles asked outright.

That question caught her off guard.

"Taking my witness to identify my Jane Doe." She should've told him that it was none of his business but being uncooperative wouldn't get her very far and she did have to face Charles at work. Their relationship was on bad enough footing as it was and she didn't want to make it worse. She decided to play innocent. "Why? What's up?"

"I think we both know." Charles shot daggers at her with his eyes.

"That only makes one of us and it's not me." She kept her voice calm and even.

"Mitchell is my case, Cordon." He would only use her last name to let her know just how angry he was. As though his charging bull routine hadn't already done the trick.

"Understood, Charles." She refused to play at his game. Using his first name was meant to remind him that they were on personal terms, a fact he seemed to have conveniently forgotten.

"I'll take you to the chief if I hear you're inserting yourself in one of my cases." Charles's threat didn't scare her.

"I'd do the same if the situation were reversed," she said.

"Well, I'm not digging around in yours so you have nothing to worry about." He didn't care about her asking T-Rex a few questions this morning. This was personal because she was with Deacon Kent. It might've been a mistake to bring him to the diner. To be fair, Charles didn't normally come here and that was one of the reasons she liked the place so much.

Leah glanced around and saw that her table had become somewhat of a show. If people stared any harder, she'd have to start selling tickets.

"Keep it that way," Charles muttered.

"Or what?" Deacon seemed to have hit his limit. His voice was calm but there was an underlying threat there.

Charles seemed to pick up on it, too. He also seemed to know when he was beat. "I don't have a problem with you. This is work talk, which was why I wanted to take it outside in the first place so as not to bother anyone else."

"Work talk? Really? Because it sounds personal to me," Deacon said. "I'd never talk to a coworker like that without expecting some backlash and I sure as hell would show more respect."

His voice might be calm and collected but his message was clear: back off.

Charles took a physical step backward. "Where do I know your name from?"

"Probably from my family business, Kent Ranch," Deacon said. His last name was powerful. Leah realized the full impact of it when Charles's demeanor changed. A flash of something—fear?—crossed his eyes. The Kent name opened doors. It was known by everyone in Texas and that most likely meant politicians, too.

Since the police chief reported to the mayor who reported to the governor, Charles seemed to realize the magnitude of the stink a Kent could create in a politically charged situation. Charles had enough sense to back down.

He put his hands up as though in surrender. "No harm. No foul."

DEACON HAD NO designs on Leah. He'd stand up for any person being bullied. Not that Leah was a wilting flower or needed his help. She'd made it clear that she could take care of herself. Still, he sensed this guy had the upper hand where they worked and Deacon couldn't sit back and watch the guy throw his weight around.

Plus, he saw jealousy for what it was. A stab of it hit him the second he'd realized that Charles Dougherty and Leah had gone out. He had no idea the extent of their relationship, but it was pretty damn clear that Leah had ended it and Charles was still licking his wounds.

Watching the man apologize before he excused himself gave Deacon no satisfaction, considering he didn't like the fact she'd dated the guy at all. That thought sat sour in Deacon's gut and there was no reason for it.

Charles was clear of the building before Deacon reclaimed his seat. Sunny had brought their plates over and set them down the minute Charles had turned toward the door.

"We dated," Leah finally said.

"I know."

"It was obvious, wasn't it?" She pushed scrambled eggs around on her plate.

"I'd have to be blind not to see it." Deacon didn't like the feeling of jealousy hammering him. It was out of place. The detective could date anyone she wanted. It wasn't his business.

"It ended months ago, but—"

"You don't owe me any explanations," Deacon interrupted. Damn, his armor was up.

"I know," she said quickly. Too quickly. A red blush heated her cheeks. It was beautiful and more than a little sexy. But it wasn't something Deacon should have allowed himself to notice under the circumstances. "I think I just want to say it out loud for myself. I mean, I'm not sure why I ever went out with him in the first place." She looked everywhere but at Deacon.

"We all make mistakes," he said, giving her an out.

"This one affects my career, you know? And I need my job now more than ever." She pushed hash browns around with her fork.

"Why did you become a detective?" There was an air to her that made him think she came from family money.

"To upset my parents." She broke into a smile despite the heavier conversation a few minutes ago. "At least, that's what they'd tell you."

Was this a rebellious rich girl? Of course, people could say something similar about Deacon. He'd made no secret out of sowing wild oats until he'd met Jackie, a single mother, and had changed his wild ways.

"You don't strike me as the insubordinate type," he said. "Don't they see the impact you make in the community with your job?"

"Apparently, I am." She rolled her eyes. "And no. They haven't agreed with anything I've done since I dropped off the debate team in favor of staying in my room alone."

He couldn't imagine having a family that didn't support his decisions. The Kents had their problems but they stuck together. "Sounds lonely."

That comment struck a chord based on the way she flinched. Hell, he hadn't meant to make her uncomfortable.

"I got used to it." She scraped her two front teeth across her bottom lip. "After I lost my best friend, I didn't really care about hanging out. You know? I was in high school and it seemed like all anyone could think about was who was hosting the next party. None of that ever really mattered to me and especially not after losing Millie. Her real name was Mildred and she hated it. She thought it made her sound old, so she went by Millie." Her eyes had a lost quality when she spoke about her friend and Deacon could relate. "Long story short, my parents said I was depressed after Millie died. They thought a therapist could *fix* me. But I just changed after that experience. Nothing was the same after that. You know?" She seemed to catch herself as she glanced up at him and blushed. "I'm sorry. I didn't mean to unload my family problems on you."

He liked that she'd confided in him, told him something real about herself. And maybe it was the all-too-familiar pain of losing someone that had drawn him to the detective in the first place.

"I'm sorry you had to go through that. No one should and especially not someone so young. I can imagine that would change the way you looked at life, at what was important, from a young age." He looked into her serious eyes and wondered if they'd ever been carefree. Life-changing moments like those altered people. Leah had been through hell, make no mistake about it. Deacon could read between the lines. The detective's friend most likely had been murdered, and the loss, the isolation had driven her to a career in law enforcement. Deacon knew from his sheriff cousin that everyone who worked in the field had a story. Some were more dramatic than others, but each had a story to tell about why they'd been drawn to the job.

He shouldn't let knowing hers crack the casing around his heart. He shouldn't listen to the voice telling him to comfort her. He shouldn't take her hand in his, but he did.

After a few seconds, Deacon withdrew his hand.

Leah blinked up at him and then asked, "How do you feel about jailhouse coffee?"

Chapter Seven

Deacon needed a mental slap as he paid the bill and walked into the frigid morning air. A few minutes ago when Leah's hand had been in his and he felt the smooth creamy skin of her delicate wrist, he'd had a few unholy thoughts. His gaze had dipped down to her lips...and he'd had to catch himself right then.

At least he was in good working condition again. After Jackie's death, he hadn't had much desire to date. He'd been out with a few women but could admit to himself that he was going through the motions.

Leah spun around and checked her watch. "It's still early, so we can make it to the jail in fifteen minutes from here."

Deacon wouldn't argue with a woman who drove around on these streets every day as part of her job. He hopped into his truck and followed her to the Tarrant County Correctional Center. The downtown building with an all-brick facade could easily be confused with a regular nine-to-five office. It was also one of the tallest buildings in Fort Worth, thereby hard to miss.

He pulled into the parking spot next to Leah and hopped out of his truck. She wheeled around the front of her sedan and stopped in front of him.

"I'll wait outside while you talk to Elijah Henry. I'm hoping your family name and influence pulls enough weight to get past the desk officer. If you get in, ask him where he was two nights ago. See if you can get a feel for whether you think he's the type. This is a violent crime and it would take some calculation on his part. Just get him talking and find out everything he knows." She touched his forearm and he ignored the electric current shooting up his arm. "Thank you, Deacon."

Deacon didn't push his luck by touching her back.

"When you go inside, ask for—"

"I know how to get past the front desk," he said.

She nodded and he headed inside.

"How can I help you?" The deputy working the desk didn't stand. She was of petite build with mousy brown hair in a tight ponytail. Her hair was pulled back so tightly that he instantly thought about Olympic gymnasts. All that was missing was glitter eyeshadow. She had the same intense focus as she looked at him.

"I'm here to see Elijah Henry." Deacon leaned his elbow on the counter. He'd been told that he had charm in spades and he didn't mind using it to his advantage on occasion.

The deputy's brown eyes widened for a split second before she let her fingers dance across the keyboard. She stared at the monitor. "What's your name?"

"Deacon Kent."

As it happened with most people, his last name got her attention.

"Of Kent Ranch?" She blinked up at him.

He nodded. That seemed to be all she needed by way of confirmation. Understanding lit her eyes as she seemed to connect the dots of who he was related to. "Since I'm in town, my cousin asked if I could stop by and ask Mr. Henry a few questions. He's hoping you'll agree out of professional courtesy."

She cocked her head to the side, which meant she was considering his request.

"Mr. Henry isn't expecting you, is he?" she asked.

"No."

"I'll have to see if he's allowed visitors before I can let you back, sir," she warned.

"Tell him I have information that will help his case." He flashed a smile and her cheeks flushed.

"Yes, sir." She disappeared behind a wall, leaving her post abandoned. There were cameras in every corner and most likely another deputy behind said wall in case someone decided to be stupid and try to break a friend or family member out of county lockup.

Deacon waited for a solid ten minutes before she returned. He stayed rooted to his spot, relaxing his arms at his sides in a show of trust. There was no need to set the deputy on edge or make her afraid that if she messed up she'd get a call from the mayor's office.

"Follow me." She came around the counter and to the door. She badged them inside and led him down a metal block corridor. This place reminded him of his small-town high school, only the walls were without the butcher paper covered with *rah-rah* and *Go Jayhawks* for the name of their football team.

His thoughts shifted back to the homicide detective in the parking lot, to the fact that wanting to kiss her had been a physical ache. Where the hell had that come from? It wasn't like Deacon didn't date around. Some might say he enjoyed women a little too much before Jackie, but he made damn certain the feeling was mutual or he didn't go there with anyone. He would never date a person who didn't have the same goals as him—a good time with even better sex. Deacon wasn't in the field for emotional attachment and that was probably why the detective was getting under his skin. She was someone he could see himself dating seriously, and Deacon didn't do serious with anyone, not anymore. Sure, a couple of his brothers had found what seemed to be genuine happiness with the opposite sex. Deacon tugged at his collar, thinking about settling down. He'd had a similar feeling when he'd considered asking Jackie to marry him. He thought about the words people used to describe marriage. Why people called it settling down. Because that's the direction his life would turn if he made a commitment to anyone, he thought. They never called it settling up and that was reason enough for Deacon to avoid it.

His thoughts shifted to the present when the deputy stopped in front of an interview room. There was a table with two metal chairs sitting opposite each other. A door to Deacon's back led to eventual freedom if an escapee could get through it and two other sets of metal doors. There were no windows but there was a two-way mirror on one wall and he was certain there'd be someone sitting on the other side of it listening in to the conversation.

"Have a seat and Mr. Henry will be with you

in a few moments," the deputy said like Deacon was sitting in the dentist's office, waiting for his teeth to be cleaned.

Deacon thanked her and she beamed at him before leaving the room. He knew that smile. He'd seen it a hundred times before. Under the right conditions, it led to flirtation, which sometimes led to grabbing a bite to eat, which under the best of circumstances led to incredible sex. He had no interest in the deputy and only part of that had to do with her looks. She wasn't bad looking. He wondered how much his reaction had to do with the intelligent and beautiful detective sitting in her vehicle outside. Smart and pretty with a body made for sex, Leah Cordon should have been his type. But the conversation he'd overheard on the trail with what sounded like her sitter meant she came with a kid. And the last time he'd gotten serious with someone who had a kid…

Either way, Deacon wasn't ready to settle. Leah deserved more. Her kid deserved better. Even though Deacon no longer wanted a family of his own, the institution was still sacred to him. Besides, there was a father out there somewhere who wouldn't appreciate another man stepping in his shoes. So, when Deacon's attraction to the detective started hitting big time again, he needed to remind himself of that fact.

He'd had a pregnancy scare once despite using a condom. Even though he hadn't been ready for his own kid at the time, he knew then that he would have figured out a way to get ready.

Damn, that was almost a decade ago. The memory still burned.

The door facing Deacon opened and a midthirties-ish man in an orange jumpsuit, hands and ankles shackled, walked in, a deputy beside him. Elijah Henry was about five feet nine inches tall with long greasy brown hair. A cigarette was tucked behind his right ear. He was thin and willowy. His expression was a mix of shock, fear and general freaking out.

Henry's gaze honed in on Deacon and he seemed to be searching his memory bank for recognition. The deputy deposited the guy in the chair across from Deacon.

The deputy looked at Deacon. "Someone will be listening to your conversation. It's illegal to pass anything to an inmate and is a punishable offense. This room has dual cameras. Mr. Henry will be searched upon exit, and if a weapon or illegal drug is found on his person, you'll be held on suspicion until your case is heard by a grand jury. Do you understand?"

"I'm clear on the rules." Deacon thanked the deputy. The man was doing his job.

On the table in between Deacon and Elijah Henry sat an ashtray and a pack of matches.

Elijah sat on the edge of the seat, his hands clasped with elbows positioned against the table. He leaned forward. "I'm sorry, man. Do I know you?"

"I'm afraid not," Deacon said.

"Are you my lawyer? Because this is crazy, man. They're trying to pin a murder on me and there ain't no way I would do that to another person."

"I'm not your legal counsel." Before Deacon could explain why he was there, Elijah shifted in his seat.

"Then who are you?" A flash of defensiveness said he was concerned Deacon was related to the victim.

"I might be able to help you but I need your cooperation." Deacon watched as a look of relief physically washed over the man. His shoulders slumped forward and he put his hands on the table.

"I didn't do nothing wrong this time," Elijah said.

Deacon figured the man for a drunk. He needed a good rehab program, not a stint in jail. But Deacon could get to that later. Right now, he sized Elijah up physically and it didn't make sense that a guy this slight could subdue a woman without anyone realizing, kill her, chop off her foot and leave the body in the shrubs with only one set of deep footprints leading to the crime scene.

"These guys have it all wrong. I wasn't nowhere near the—" Elijah stopped short of finishing. He pulled the smoke from behind his ear with shaky hands. "You mind?"

Deacon shook his head.

Elijah lit the cigarette and drew in a big drag. He blew out smoke in a rush, flooding the space between them, but it also looked like the first time he'd really breathed.

"Why would you help me?" he asked, fidgeting with the matchbook, twirling it between his fingers nervously.

"Because I think you're innocent, and if they don't catch the right man, someone else will die." It was the gospel truth.

"I tried to tell 'em they had the wrong guy. I didn't do nothing wrong." He stopped long enough to take another pull of his smoke. "But they won't listen. Said they have a witness who saw me and that this will all go a lot easier if I confess. I can't admit to something I never done."

"Where were you the night before last?" Deacon couldn't see someone of Elijah's size pulling off the crime that had been committed.

"I was out and about." Elijah shrugged.

"Did anyone see you?" Deacon asked.

"I mean, people had to have seen me. I like to walk around at night and I'd gotten into a huff with Lacey." He seemed to realize that Deacon wouldn't know who she was. "She's my girl. We've been dating for a month. I know that because I forgot and she got all upset about me missing our anniversary."

"The two of you had words and then you left to get some air," Deacon said.

"That's what happened to a T." Elijah made a *T* with his hands as though for emphasis. "I didn't hurt that woman."

"Did you know her?" Deacon asked.

"Not personally. I used to be a janitor at her building a year or so ago but we never talked none." Deacon was beginning to see the connection. The DA would go after a retaliation crime. He'd most likely say that she'd turned her nose up at the janitor and he'd been biding his time.

"How long ago was that?"

"A year and a few months, I reckon. It was before I got on disability." Elijah seemed to be counting out the months in his head. His face brightened. "Fourteen months ago."

"Why'd you get put on disability?" He'd noticed a slight limp when Elijah walked in, now that he really thought about it.

"Hurt my hip after falling from the roof," he said.

"Will you be able to work again?" Deacon thought about the possible connection to Elijah's limp and having something taken from him.

"Doc says we'll know after my next surgery," Elijah confessed.

Deacon stood. He'd bet anything this guy wasn't the killer. He was too weak physically to pull off the crime. There'd been no mention of a bad leg and it would've come up based on the footprints leading up to the scene of the crime. One foot would've left a deeper impression. "Thank you for your time, Mr. Henry."

"Hold on a second." Elijah's jumpiness returned full force. "You said you could help me. If I don't get home, Lacey will think I hit the bars and ran off with one of 'em dancers."

"You've already told me what I need to know to help you. You haven't been arraigned yet so no lawyer has been assigned to your case. I'll have the judge get you out of here," Deacon informed him.

"You would do that for me?"

"For justice. If you're in here, no one's looking for the real murderer." The statement seemed to satisfy Elijah. He rocked his head.

"I hope they get that guy. He's twisted," Elijah stated.

That was the truth.

"Thank you for your help, sir," Elijah said.

"Take care of that hip." An unsettled feeling came over Deacon. All he could think about was getting back to the detective.

LEAH DIDN'T LIKE the looks of a white four-door sedan parked across the street. The sun was up and from this angle it reflected off the front windshield so that she couldn't get a look at the driver.

Is that why he'd parked there? Did he know? Or was it just a random person who'd pulled off the street in order to take a call?

She checked her phone again. No call. No text. Nothing from Deacon.

Her heart skipped a few beats when she saw him walking toward her. Out of the corner of her eye, she noticed the white sedan backing out of its spot.

Tension caused her to grip her phone so tightly she felt like she could almost bend the metal. A hit of adrenaline spiked as she thought about the driver of the sedan trying to do something to Deacon. She tried to calm her racing pulse as she replaced her cell with her Glock.

The white sedan drove in the opposite direction. It was too soon to sigh in relief. The vehicle had been too far away to read the plates and had disappeared before she'd had a chance to call it in as suspicious. Besides, it could've just been a driver pulling into an empty spot in order to make or take a phone call. Her nerves were on edge but she reminded herself not to jump at every loud noise.

She exited her vehicle as Deacon neared. Her stomach flipped like a schoolgirl's with a crush on the high school quarterback.

"What did you find out?" she asked, leaning her hip against her sedan.

The way his eyes seemed to take her in, appreciating her, wasn't helping with her attraction.

"Your hunch is right. He didn't do it," Deacon said.

She knew it. "What did he say?"

"It wasn't so much that. Of course, he claimed to be innocent. His hair was too long and too unkempt. He would've left DNA all over the crime scene. Plus, he was too small." Deacon folded his arms and stood in an athletic stance, showing that he was confident in his assessment. "The man couldn't sit still and there was real fear in his eyes."

"You sure he wasn't just afraid of spending the rest of his life behind bars?" It was a fair question, but based on Deacon's body language she didn't expect him to change his opinion.

"I considered that at first. Here's the thing.

Henry is thin. No muscles. He'd have had to have something to overpower Jillian Mitchell, subdue her and then do what he did to her ankle. This guy doesn't strike me as powerful enough to pull it off."

His assessment had been carefully thought out. "What about an alibi?"

"He got in a fight with his girlfriend and took a walk, so she can't verify his whereabouts. Henry is a drunk and a criminal but he's not a butcher." Deacon seemed sure of himself.

"I get that he's not strong but someone put him near the scene." They couldn't overlook an eyewitness.

Without a weapon the case was flimsy, but if a detective could squeeze a confession out of Henry—which was what was likely happening in this case—the murder weapon would take a back seat. And especially to someone with a history like his.

"Henry is messy. He looks like he drinks too much, maybe does a little bit of smoke when he has the extra cash. The guy who is butchering our cattle is methodical. He doesn't leave DNA evidence. He's not haphazard. I'm envisioning someone clean-cut who possibly has something to lose by being found out. This guy is going to great lengths to ensure he can't be traced back to these animals. He's intelligent and calculating.

Henry is a greasy hippie with a bad temper and a history of violence against women," he said. "He reacts in the moment."

"I'm impressed." The man had thought this through carefully. "You'd make an excellent detective."

She thought she heard him mumble that he was still trying to figure out who the hell he was. He'd said it so low that she almost hadn't caught it so she didn't comment. It was hard to believe that a man who'd had his entire life handed to him on a silver platter would feel that way.

Hold on a minute. Was that the problem?

Leah could relate to the feeling of being trapped that came with parents who'd planned out her entire life. Her parents had tried to force her down a different path and yet she couldn't imagine another life. The tension in her family dynamic made it easier to walk away, but what if she'd been close to her parents? What if she'd respected them? Disappointing them would have been a physical punch.

Was that why Deacon Kent had those tormented eyes? "Can I ask you a personal question?"

Deacon's eyebrow shot up as he nodded.

"What happened to you?"

Chapter Eight

"You're not asking about the ranch, are you?" Deacon didn't talk about his personal affairs with anyone, not even his siblings. He'd always been the quiet one.

"No." She studied him and he felt like she was looking right through him.

"I'd rather discuss Elijah Henry," he said honestly.

"I see your points and I agree with you wholeheartedly," she said. Observing the detective standing there, leaning a slender hip against her vehicle, brought emotions to the surface that Deacon had no desire to deal with. Again, he reminded himself that *any* woman with a kid was off-limits. Losing two people he loved—albeit in very different ways—was one of those norecover situations. Trust him.

Deacon shoved those thoughts down deep. A sense of pride hit him in the chest that she respected his thinking. That's as far as he could let it go. "What's next?"

"You met the lead detective on the case." Her cheeks flushed with embarrassment and the natural red blush was even more attractive.

Way to keep those feelings in check, Deacon.

"Does he think he's already arrested his man?" Charles Dougherty was a bull in a china shop. There was no way he would change his mind on a case once it was set. Deacon had dealt with that type of person before.

"That's my impression." She hesitated, shifting her weight from one foot to the other. "He's not a hundred percent jerk and he's not a bad detective."

"He's just not especially thrilled that you don't trust his judgment," he finished for her. "Us going to the coroner made it clear to him that we have questions about the case and the suspect."

"That's my trail. I jog there every night at about that same time. I can't—won't!—look over my shoulder every time I put on my jogging shoes." She said that last part so emphatically that it could only mean there was a story there.

Her gaze locked on to his and he could see fire in her eyes. He saw something else, too, and it was dangerous as hell because he was barely containing his attraction as it was.

She took a step toward him, eyes on him as though asking permission or maybe it was just hope that she wouldn't be denied.

There was no way he could turn her down. If she started something, he would finish it. It was already taking all his willpower not to haul her against his chest and capture that little freckle a fraction of an inch above her top lip in the corner.

"Deacon. Would it be a bad idea to get any closer?" She never broke eye contact. Her voice was a little deeper, a little sexier.

"Yep."

She brought her hands up to his chest where she splayed her fingers. He could feel her hands trembling with the same need welling up inside of him. Electricity pulsed as he dropped his hands to either side of her hips. He didn't pull her toward him and he didn't push her away. Logically, he knew he should take a step back but his body didn't listen to reason. He brought his hands up to her shoulders and then he caressed the back of her neck.

Even with a foot and a half of space between them, he could feel heat radiating from her. She fisted his shirt, her knuckles against his chest now. Her pulse raced, thumping against his thumb at the base. The tempo was a pretty darn close match to his.

"Kiss me, Deacon," was all she said, was all she needed to say as she looped her arms around his neck and tunneled her fingers in his hair.

Deacon took in a slow breath. There was a point when he could have stopped himself from moving forward, from doing what they both knew would take them down a path neither seemed ready to take.

But then she looked up at him and her eyes were all glittery with desire. There was something else there, too. Fear? Was she afraid that he wasn't attracted to her?

Deacon took a step toward her, dipped his head and brushed his mouth against hers. The taste of dark roast coffee still on her lips. He took in a deep breath, heady with the scent that was her, a mix of citrus and flowers and fresh-from-a-spring-rain clean.

She parted her lips, an invitation to deepen the kiss.

Deacon thrust his tongue inside her mouth and swallowed her mewl. He dropped his hands to loop around her waist and she pressed her body flush with his.

In the space of a few seconds, they'd gone from reasonable restraint to hands touching, mouths fusing and bodies pressed together. He could feel her generous breasts against his chest and all blood flew south. He was hit with a thunderclap of need—a feeling so out of the blue it was like lightning striking on a sunny beach day with not a cloud in the sky.

Okay, sure, he'd been attracted to the smart and beautiful detective from the get-go. There was no denying that. He wanted to believe it was his sense of chivalry that had him making sure she was all right after the scare the other night. But if he were being honest, it was something much more primal than that.

Leah Cordon was no pushover but she awakened protective instincts he'd long since believed were dead.

The only thing he could think about now was how amazing she felt pressed up against him. Her soft curves to his hard body. Her hands dropped to his shoulders and she dug her fingers in. If kissing her was this all-consuming, he could only imagine what sex would be like...

Hold on, right there. He needed to stop this right now. The detective was most likely in a vulnerable state and needed reassurance that life would still go on. She'd been traumatized, whether she'd admit it or not, by Jillian Mitchell's murder.

Deacon almost had himself talked into pulling back when she did it for them. Her eyes were wild and her lips so damn inviting. Her breathing was as ragged as his.

"We can't do that again," she said.

"I know." Well, hell. If they agreed this couldn't happen again, he might as well enjoy it for right now. He brought his hand up and tilted her head for better access. "Just so we're clear, this is the last time."

She cracked a smile.

"Agreed."

This time, he kissed her so thoroughly he couldn't be sure how long they stood there in the parking lot making out. But he was certain that he'd never experienced a kiss like the ones they were sharing.

When they broke apart, she leaned into him like she was listening to his rapid heartbeat through his rib cage. And he held her, reminding his heart that this was a temporary situation.

Which worked right until the point she tugged at his shirt and looked up at him with eyes that said she wanted him.

DEACON STOPPED THE next kiss before Leah was ready. But she also knew he'd made the right call. She leaned into him until her head rested against him. She could hear his heart pound under his ribs; the rhythm matched her staccato tempo. All her senses were heightened.

It was oddly comforting to listen, so she stood there. It should have felt awkward to kiss a practical stranger, but it hadn't. There was no way she could let her feelings run away from her with Deacon. Seeing Charles at the diner was a stark reminder of how a relationship could deteriorate in an instant, and of the consequences when it did. With Charles, she was now uncomfortable at work. He had a higher rank than her and could make her life miserable. A fact he seemed to realize and acted on.

The feeling she had with Deacon was different than that. The scale was off. There was something about Deacon that made her think she wouldn't survive losing him. It was odd because, again, they'd barely just met. Although, the shot she had taken to the heart made her realize instantly that there was something different about Deacon Kent.

Besides, he'd be a good ally to have and one she couldn't afford to lose because of overwrought hormones. Amazing sex with a man she deeply cared about was something she'd never experienced.

"What happened in your past that makes you so afraid?" he asked quietly in her ear, so quietly it wasn't more than a breeze.

Part of her wanted to open up and tell him the horror she'd lived since losing her best friend, the sadness she felt in her parents turning their backs on her. And then the loss she felt when her husband, Wyatt, had died. But that's where she stopped. What good would come from talking about any of those things? Feeling good came when she could give answers to families, real answers to what had happened in a loved one's last hours. That's all she could let herself think about.

"Jillian Mitchell's family deserves to know the truth about what happened to her. She has a mother and father, a brother. They deserve to know who took her from them or they'll never recover." She thought about Millie. Leah wondered how much of that fateful night caused her parents to shut down on her. Never knowing what had actually happened to her best friend had changed Leah. Had it changed them, too?

Everyone dealt with grief differently. Did they realize how easily that could've been her out that night? Did they know how close she'd come to meeting up with her best friend? If she hadn't been studying for finals so hard and then fell asleep on her desk, waiting for the meet-up time, she might've saved her best friend's life.

Her parents had never understood that. The self-blame. The grief. When she couldn't *buck up* a year later, they had seemed to give up on her ever trying.

But those were things she didn't talk about with anyone. Surprisingly, she wanted to tell

Deacon. It was too much, too soon and they had another case to focus on. Find the answers to the Mitchell murder and then she'd tell him.

Leah's cell buzzed.

She avoided eye contact with Deacon. She knew better than to look at him when she was feeling so vulnerable—a state she didn't normally visit and sure as hell didn't wallow in.

"It's from Charles." She stared at the text on the screen.

Deacon's muscles tensed and she wondered if it was because he realized Charles was having a hard time letting go or if he just didn't like the man.

Either way, he wasn't going to be thrilled with the message on her screen. Deacon Kent's fingerprints have been lifted from the crime scene.

Chapter Nine

Leah tilted her phone's screen toward Deacon. He read the message. "Why would they go back and check for prints at the crime scene?"

"Great question," she said, looking at him sympathetically. "And especially since you had on gloves."

"I took those off."

"Right."

Deacon saw through Charles Dougherty. He and Leah had obviously been in a serious relationship and the man was a sore loser. The breakup had to have been recent for him to still be licking his wounds. Deacon had to ask an important question. Could being with Leah jeopardize his getting information about the crime?

The next text that came read, Bring him in to talk to the chief and then keep clear of him if you care about your career.

Based on Leah's expression as she read the

text, the warning was about as welcome as fire ants overrunning a picnic.

"I'm sorry he's making this personal." There was sincerity in her serious eyes as she blinked up at him. "It's probably best if you go in to the station on your own and explain your side of the story to Chief Dillinger. He won't like the fact that you visited the crime scene or spoke to Henry but he's reasonable and it's understandable what you're doing to solve the crimes against your animals. I won't tell you to lie about going to the morgue. I signed in but left your name off any paperwork."

"I believe in telling the truth," he said. For some reason he cared that she knew he was an honest man.

"Being with me is going to make you Charles's target." That much was certain.

"I don't back down from bullies." He took her hand in his. "What's your next move?"

"Explain myself to my boss and hope for the best," she admitted. "Charles is being a jerk and he's trying to back me down."

Deacon didn't want to say his impression of Charles out loud. It involved a few choice words. If Deacon could face off with Charles one-on-one, he wouldn't hesitate. The fact that Charles had gone behind their backs and spoken to someone in charge in order to get her in trouble for her association with Deacon said all he needed to know about the man's character.

"Seems to me we should head to the station right away. The longer the chief has to let his imagination run wild, the worse it'll be for you." Deacon put his hand on the small of her back and walked her to the driver's side of her vehicle.

She stopped at the opened door, took his hand and tugged him toward her without saying a word.

He couldn't help himself. He kissed her one more time, swearing it was the last. This time, he captured that freckle after she bit down on his bottom lip. His blood got going again, heating as it fired through his veins. The detective was sexy. Her intelligence skyrocketed her to a whole new level of attraction.

She has a kid. Deacon would remind himself of the fact a hundred times an hour if he had to in order to keep his attraction in check.

On the ride to the station, Deacon must've repeated that mantra four dozen times. He also called his friend, Mayor Shield, to give him a heads-up on the situation. Deacon parked next to her vehicle and exited his.

With a look of fortitude and a deep breath, she led him into the brick one-story. There were twin glass doors up the set of stairs leading into the lobby area. Leah badged them inside after greeting the officer at the front desk.

The chief's office was at the back of the old schoolhouse-looking building. There was more glass but his office also had mini blinds in order to shut everyone out, which seemed odd. Why build a glass office if the blinds were going to be closed most of the time?

The slats were open enough to see the chief sitting at his desk, staring at his computer screen.

Leah knocked.

The chief looked to be in his early fifties and in peak physical fitness. He glanced up and frowned as he waved them inside.

"Sir, this is Deacon Kent," Leah said, stepping aside as though presenting Deacon.

Recognition of the last name flashed behind the middle-aged man's serious blue eyes. His hair was mostly gray but there were remnants of the blond streaks from his younger days. He wore the expression of a man who had the world on his shoulders. He was a buttoned-up guy.

Deacon stepped forward and stretched out his hand. The chief took the offering in a vigorous shake. The job was political in many ways and Deacon wondered if the handshake was natural to Dillinger or if he'd learned it for the job. None of which mattered if the guy was actually good at what he did.

Assessing the situation, Deacon figured going in throwing his weight around wouldn't get the results he wanted from this meeting and could end up getting Leah in more trouble.

"I apologize for any inconvenience, Chief," Deacon started.

Dillinger nodded. "You want to have a seat?"

The chief was either being polite or figured this was going to take a while. Or maybe he was just feeling Deacon out.

"I'm okay standing," Deacon said, making it clear he didn't intend to be there for long. The chief reported to the mayor and Mayor Shield was a longtime family friend of the Kent family. Dillinger most likely knew this.

"Would you like to explain why your prints were found at my crime scene?" Dillinger got straight to the point.

"As a matter of fact, I would. I visited the scene the night after the murder." Deacon paused out of respect for Jillian Mitchell. He lowered his voice. "My deepest sympathy goes to the Mitchell family."

The chief acknowledged the moment of silence. "Can I ask what you thought you'd find?"

"Are you aware of the killings on my family's ranch?" Deacon asked.

"The mayor briefed me a few minutes ago."

The chief's voice was steady. If he'd been intimidated or offended, he didn't show it. But then in a city the size of Fort Worth, the man had probably seen and heard almost everything. A chief in a city with that many residents would also know the political aspects of the job.

Deacon owed Shield a thank-you call because he had a feeling this meeting would be going a lot differently if the mayor hadn't intervened.

"My fear is that the killer could be escalating. From what I read in the news the other morning, this case seemed like exactly that was happening. I wanted to help," Deacon said.

"Why not call my office?"

It was a reasonable question. "I wasn't sure I had anything to say yet."

"And now?" This got the chief's attention.

"I'm convinced it's not the same guy."

Dillinger looked startled. "How so?"

"Our guy hacks the left hoof and then leaves the heifer to bleed out, like he's taunting us. Jillian Mitchell's right foot was cut clean off."

"I have a suspect behind bars," the chief said.

He couldn't share the part about his knowing there was no murder weapon recovered. "How strong is the case?"

The chief didn't respond, which meant he knew he'd have to release Henry.

"You have a scared man with a rap sheet in lockup who didn't commit the crime," Deacon said.

"Are you interfering with my investigation?" The chief's chest practically puffed out. Politics or no, he wouldn't appreciate someone from the outside interfering in his territory.

"I spoke to Henry to see if there was a connection. I'm a concerned citizen, trying to stop a man from butchering cattle or worse, women. It was never my intention to get in the way of any of your people. But can I ask you this? Why would a detective return to a crime scene and look for prints after he'd already done so?" It was worth putting out there.

LEAH STOOD THERE, head bowed, giving nothing away of her reaction to the exchange between Deacon and the chief. She knew better.

The chief was a reasonable man. He'd see the logic.

"I don't discuss ongoing murder investigations with citizens no matter how much influence he or she might have," the chief said after a moment of contemplation.

"Then this meeting is over." Deacon stood his ground and part of Leah wanted to clap. "Unless I need an attorney, in which case—"

The chief waved him off. "That's not necessary, Mr. Kent. I appreciate your coming here on your own free will so promptly. I'm sure you can appreciate the fact that a woman has been murdered on my watch and I don't take that lightly."

"Believe me, I'm clear on that." Deacon's tone left no room for doubt.

"Thank you for your time." The chief stuck out his hand between them.

Deacon took the offering.

"If anything comes up, will you let us know?" The chief seemed to know Deacon wouldn't let this go until he had answers.

"Will do, Chief." Deacon turned to walk out.

"Leah, stick around after Mr. Kent leaves."

DREAD SETTLED ON Leah's shoulders like a heavy wet blanket in the cold. Nothing in her wanted to stick around and speak to the chief. Everything in her wanted to walk out that door behind Deacon. "I'll just see Mr. Kent out."

The chief nodded.

Leah walked Deacon out to the parking lot.

"I'm sorry about Charles," she said.

"It's pretty clear he won't let this go. I won't have my family name dragged through the mud over his jealousy." Deacon meant those words. Leah could see it in his clear gray eyes.

"What makes you think that's the problem?"

"The way he looked at you. His anger." Deacon raked his hand through his thick hair. "No one gets that frustrated with someone when they don't know the details of a situation unless they still have feelings for them. How long ago did the two of you date?"

She didn't want to talk about Charles with Deacon Kent. But she took in a deep breath and dove in anyway. "It's been months since the breakup. There wasn't much on my side of the relationship to begin with but I'm starting to see that the time we spent together meant more to him than I realized. He's been going through a lot emotionally and I guess so have I." And that was as much as she was ready to say about it. "I better get back inside. The chief is waiting."

Deacon took a step toward her and dipped his head down to kiss her.

All willpower to fight against her growing feelings for him exploded. Her fingertips tingled with the desire to touch him again, to get lost in his hair as he kissed her.

He hesitated as though waiting for permission before their lips touched. She pushed up to her tiptoes and pressed her mouth against his.

His hands came up to either side of her face, cupping it. Her palms flattened against his muscled chest.

The words *this can't happen* were a distant memory as his tongue delved into her mouth.

The air hummed with electricity, charging around them.

Rational thought disappeared and all she could focus on was the moment happening between them.

He pulled back first and looked in her eyes.

"You'll be all right?" There was a protectiveness to his voice that sent a rocket of warmth spiraling through her. Leah could take care of herself and she didn't need anyone to stand up for her. But it was nice for someone else to have her back for a change. Even in the world of police work, which was a family in its own right, she always felt on the fringe. She'd chosen this life and didn't regret a minute of it. With her family background, which everyone in the department seemed to clue in on from day one, it was always going to be an uphill battle. Females from The Heights didn't go into police work. They got into the *right* colleges after prep school, took six-figure jobs or important volunteer positions after graduating. What had her mother said? *Be the person who makes policy, not enforces it. Any idiot with a gun could do that.*

Leave it to Mother to insult Leah and an entire profession in one fell swoop.

"He's frustrated now but it'll blow over." At least she hoped it would. Ruining her career wasn't high on her list of things to do.

Saying goodbye and walking away from Deacon stung more than it should have. A strange part of her wanted to turn around and tell him she'd call him later. She told herself that he'd been a comfort and that was the feeling she was hanging on to. Her mind railed against putting him in the friend zone and especially with the way sexual tension pinged between them every time he was near.

The chief's door was still open, so she tapped on the glass. She threw her shoulders back in order to fake confidence and forced herself to clear her throat to get the chief's attention.

Chief Dillinger glanced up from the screen he'd been studying like he was in the middle of taking the MCAT and his future depended on the outcome.

"Come in." He had that stern voice that he'd probably used with perps when he was on the street.

"Sir, I apologize for—"

"Sit down, Cordon."

Leah took a seat opposite from him. The chair wasn't shorter like executives used to give the illusion of being taller and, therefore, more dominant. Dillinger had more height compared to most normal men. Deacon was six feet four inches, tall even by Texas standards. Dillinger didn't need to manipulate a chair to show his authority. He was a good chief.

"A senior detective has been talking about you." He stared at her as he steepled his fingers before placing them on top of his otherwise neat and clear desk.

She felt the heat from his glare.

"Detective Dougherty might've overlooked key evidence in the Mitchell case," she started before he stopped her with a hand up.

"Get to your point." His gaze narrowed.

"He has the wrong guy locked up." She hadn't spoken to the suspect but trusted Deacon's assessment. The guy's investigative and observation skills were solid.

"Did you interview Detective Dougherty's suspect?"

"No. But I jog that trail every night around the same time, sir. If the wrong man's locked up, I want to know. I have reason to believe the killer is still out there."

The chief's stare caused the temperature in the room to rise uncomfortably.

"Mr. Kent's prints were found at the crime scene," Dillinger said. "That says he's not particularly careful."

"He didn't think he had to be. The area had already been taped off. What I want to know is why a detective would bother searching for prints after that."

"Meaning?"

"Dougherty went back to lift prints a second time after he knew that Mr. Kent had been in the area," she said.

"And how did Dougherty know that?"

"I called it in." She explained that she'd been on the trail and had caught Kent there. She further explained the reason.

Dillinger hiked a brow.

She steadied herself for the blast that was coming next.

"I've spent the last ten minutes studying the case file. I agree with your assessment of the suspect in custody. I also see the possible link between Ms. Mitchell's killer and the activity on Mr. Kent's ranch. I need to be clear on what I'm about to say next. I can't have a citizen conducting his own investigation and, worse yet, prove a senior detective is letting his personal relationships color his judgment."

Leah bit back a curse. That meant the chief knew about her relationship with Dougherty.

Dillinger leaned back in his chair. "Take some time off."

"I'm okay," she quickly countered.

"That's not a request."

Chapter Ten

Leah rolled her head from side to side, trying to loosen the tension in her neck as she tied her running shoes. It had been a long day. It was nine o'clock and had been dark outside for hours already. Her conversation with the chief kept circling back in her thoughts no matter how hard she tried to shut them down and redirect.

Connor was sleeping and Riley was studying. Leah had held her son a little tighter tonight and figured her past emotions were catching up to her.

Five days was the most she'd taken off in a row since making detective. She could tell herself that it was because she was focused on getting ahead, that she had tunnel vision, and part of that would be right. The other very real part was that digging into work was easier than dealing with parents whose love came with conditions and a husband who'd died shortly after a diagnosis and short bout with illness.

They'd been married two months before the fatal news came.

The feeling of eyes watching Leah caused the hairs on her neck to prick. She glanced around, realizing she was most likely being paranoid. It didn't matter. She would never take an unnecessary risk.

She brought her hand to the butt of her holstered Glock to rest as she scanned the street. There was nothing going on and no one around. The noise was nothing more than a burst of wind shuffling around leaves across the street on the sidewalk.

Leah finished tying her shoes and stretched her hamstrings. She rolled her ankles around, keeping careful watch of her surroundings. And then she tucked her left earbud in place and cranked up "Bad Medicine" by Bon Jovi.

A few minutes later, she started off toward her trail, walking at a faster pace than usual. Eyes and ears open, she knew it would be impossible to focus on her run while the real killer was still on the loose. At least the area was hot and that would make him less likely to strike again so soon. She had no idea if her popular running trail was the target of a murderer or if he'd strike anywhere he could isolate a victim. A chill raced down her spine as she picked up speed to a light jog.

The cool night breeze toyed with her hair as she finally found her stride. It felt good to run. She thought about the rubber band around her wrist, about pulling her hair off her face, but she liked the way it felt as it whipped around in the chilly wind. Her hair down, covering her neck, kept her warmer. She'd left her jacket at home, wearing only a sweatshirt in case she needed quick access to her Glock.

The turn at Porter's Bend was a quarter of a mile away when she spotted a man sitting on the bench. Her heart gave a little flip. She knew exactly who he was. Deacon Kent.

Leah pulled the earbud from her ear and let it dangle in front of her as she made a beeline toward Deacon. "What are you doing here?"

On the bench next to him sat two cups of what looked like coffee.

"Hoping to run into you." He quirked a smile like he'd just figured out the double entendre. "Coffee?"

The warm brew would feel good in her hands. She took the offering being held up.

It was too hot to drink.

"You just got here?" It wasn't good that her routine made her so predictable in the greater sense. For now, she liked it. But if Deacon knew her schedule, then anyone could easily figure it out. Running outside in the cold had her ears and nose freezing while the rest of her was sweaty. It was strange how that worked.

"I wanted to check on you after your meeting with the chief. Make sure he didn't go too hard on you." Deacon nodded as he stood.

"Don't get up for my sake." She'd barely said the words when she realized he was cut from the kind of cloth that would make it impossible for him to sit when a lady stood next to him.

"The bench isn't all that comfortable," he said by way of explanation, but she figured it had to do with a Cowboy Code. It was another nice thing she didn't want to notice about Deacon Kent.

For a split second they just stood there in silence. He was standing so close she could smell his woodsy aftershave. She flexed the fingers on her free hand.

Eye contact was a bad idea. She knew the second their gazes met that she was in trouble again. Keeping her attraction in check with this man was proving far more difficult than she'd expected.

"Something's going on between us." Boldly, his gaze never left hers.

All she could say was, "Yes."

"The kisses—" he paused for a brief second "—they can't go anywhere."

"I know." She shouldn't have felt let down at

saying those two words out loud. They were true and she meant them on an intellectual level. Her emotions were getting the best of her. Deacon was the first man she'd been attracted to since... She should say the man she'd married but that wouldn't have been true. No man had ever made her feel the way Deacon did.

"Not because I don't want them to," he said.

"Save me the it's-me-and-not-you speech. Okay?" She would literally shrivel up right there in front of him if he recited that one. Embarrassment flamed her cheeks.

He started to explain himself, but honestly she wasn't in the mood for excuses. She put her hand up. "Seriously. I'm a grown woman. We kissed. I'm sure if we took it further, the fireworks would blow my mind. I've got a Jane Doe case I can no longer work thanks to my boss's orders of a 'vacation,' a killer on the loose on my favorite jogging trail and you're trying to track down a cattle butcher."

The chilly air was starting to penetrate her sweatshirt so she sat down on the bench. Besides, she needed to put a little distance between them. So it didn't help matters when he took a seat right next to her. He was so close their outer thighs touched.

A shiver rippled through her in sharp contrast to the heat pulsing up her leg from the contact.

"How'd it go with your boss?" Deacon asked.

"I'm on a forced vacation." She shifted her weight away from him to create some distance. There was way too much heat radiating from him and he was right. An attraction now was too much of a distraction. It was most likely so intense because he was here on a cold night, showing up just when she needed someone to lean on.

"That doesn't sound good for your career." A sharp sigh issued. "Maybe I should have a talk with Detective Dougherty."

"Won't help. In fact, that might make things worse for me." She wanted to explain her complicated history with Charles, but she also realized she and Deacon knew very little about each other. Another blast of frigid wind slammed into her and she shivered again.

Deacon took off his coat and wrapped it around her shoulders. She thanked him but he made a gesture like it was no big deal. Considering he was pretty much the only man who'd done that for her, it was.

Since she figured the best way to make Deacon run was to share a little about her life, she decided to go for it.

"I have a kid."

"Boy or girl?" He didn't seem shocked by the revelation. And then she remembered that she'd called home the other night and he must've overheard her talking to her sitter, checking on her child.

"Boy. Connor's three years old."

"My brother has young twins." He laughed and it was a deep rumble in his chest. "They're adorable but keep him hopping."

"Twins?" She couldn't hide her shock. She couldn't even imagine what that must be like, considering how much Connor kept her on her toes.

"A boy and a girl," he said.

"Wow. Just wow." Leah tried to wrap her mind around it and came up short. "He must be…tired."

She laughed despite herself.

"The ranch has been busy to say the least." Deacon's smile looked so good on him.

"Is that part of the reason you're searching for the butcher? I mean, you have a wonderful family and it sounds like lots of little ones running around." She couldn't imagine that kind of loyalty but then she'd never had siblings. "You guys are close-knit, right?"

"The butcher made his first mistake by stepping on our land. Kents are loyal to each other and to Texas. And, yes, we're close. Some days too much." He chuckled and the sound came from low in his chest again. She didn't want to notice how sexy his voice was vibrating through the crisp night air. Or the inappropriate warmth it brought. All she really wanted to do was shut down that side of her altogether like it had always been so easy to do in the past. "What about you? What about your family?"

The questions caught her off guard.

"It's just me. I mean, I have parents, of course, but we're not close." Had she already opened up too much in their previous conversation? She didn't want to go into a lengthy explanation about her parents not even knowing her son because they didn't agree with her choice in men. Or the fact, looking back, she may have confused her feelings for Wyatt for real love because her parents were so opposed to the relationship in the first place.

"They don't see your son?" There was no condemnation in his voice like she'd expected. There was disbelief.

"Not really. We go to lunch with them once a year on the day after his birthday," she admitted. A surprising shock of pain stabbed her in the chest. When she heard herself say the words out loud, it sounded lonely even to her.

"He has you and his father," Deacon said.

"I'm afraid it's just me." There was no pity in her voice. She didn't feel sorry for herself. She'd allowed Wyatt to die in peace by not telling him about his son. Wyatt would never have forgiven himself for abandoning his child—he hadn't—but he'd have never seen it that way.

"Oh." There was so much confusion communicated in that one word.

"He died without knowing he had a child on the way." The air whooshed from her lungs. She never spoke about it, and even though she took an emotional hit by doing just that, relief flooded her, too. She'd spent too much time locking up her emotions so she didn't offend anyone.

"I'm really sorry about that." There was so much sincerity in his voice.

"I knew but didn't tell him." Again, she expected judgment but found none. A rare feeling of acceptance crept over her.

"I'm sure you had a good reason."

"Wyatt was his name. His own father wasn't around and he had a lot of emotional baggage because of it. I often told him that sometimes no parent was better than two, but he'd tell me I should be grateful that I had people who cared about me." She was on the one hand. But on the other, her life had been strangely isolating with her parents around. "This won't make sense to you with your family background, but being with my parents made me feel like a third wheel. It was like they were in some kind of club that I didn't belong to."

He sat there in silence for a minute like he was contemplating her words. Maybe he did know?

"Families can be complicated," he said.

"That sure as hell describes mine." She paused a beat. "Wyatt found out he was terminal and I just couldn't let him die feeling like he'd abandoned his child. As it was, he had someone who cared about him by his side when he took his last breath. I wasn't going to ruin that for him, even though I question myself every single day for making that decision."

"Second-guessing yourself won't make the pain go away." His expression said he had firsthand knowledge of the fact. "It'll only extend it. You did right by your husband. You made the only call you could in an impossible situation. He's at peace."

A few rogue tears spilled down Leah's cheeks and she realized just how much she'd needed to hear those words. She hadn't been able to talk about her relationship with Wyatt at work because dating a coworker was bad enough and marrying one—especially one so much older than she—had garnered quite a few hall whispers when she walked by. She'd tried to pretend that she didn't notice or that it didn't hurt her feelings but she was human. Everyone wanted to feel accepted by peers.

It surprised her when Deacon thumbed away

the stray tears. Contact was welcomed, even though she knew better than to allow herself to want it.

"I'm sorry," she said quickly. Too quickly?

"Don't be." His gaze lingered and he seemed to catch himself when he broke eye contact and leaned against the bench again. A sharp breath issued a few seconds later. "We should talk about the case."

DEACON HAD HAD to catch himself before he fell into that pit again. The one that had him ignoring all the warning sirens sounding off in his head. It had only been days since they'd met and yet part of him felt like they'd known each other for most of their lives. Deacon had never been a love-at-first-sight person so the bolt of lightning that had struck him caught him way off guard. Leah Cordon needed to be hands-off. Period.

"The person who killed Jillian Mitchell could have been paying attention to the news," Leah said.

"Which either means we might be dealing with a copycat or someone who wants us to believe our butcher has moved on to women." He was grateful for the refocus. He needed to keep his attention on the case where it needed to stay. Focus was not normally a problem for Deacon. "Zach made another statement. News about the weapon has been intentionally left out of the press on our side."

"It's harder to keep that under wraps in a town this size," she said.

"Did the chief clue you in to what Charles believes?" He didn't want to talk about her ex but there was no helping it. The man was in charge of Jillian Mitchell's case.

"Dougherty believes the killer graduated to a better tool if these two cases are linked." She took a sip of coffee.

"Elijah Henry can't prove his whereabouts but that didn't mean he committed the crime. He was a janitor in the building where Jillian Mitchell worked." Leah reacted to that statement by sitting up a little straighter.

"He knew her?"

"I must've forgotten to mention that part earlier. The two might've been in the same building at the same time but they didn't keep company. They'd never shared an elevator or spoken."

"It sounds like a pretty loose association," she admitted.

"Why does Dougherty want to wrap this case up so fast?"

"Public pressure. The mayor's office is involved. This kind of brutal crime has a high profile in the community and he wants to be a hero." Her shoulders slumped. "I'm making him sound like a jerk."

"That's true of what I witnessed earlier."

"Yeah, I know. I get that." She sat there. Her gaze intensified on her coffee. "He came to me for advice when his kid got sick last year. I didn't know what to tell him but I wanted to help. I mean, I know what it's like to lose someone. Maybe not a child. I can't even imagine that horror."

Deacon went quiet.

"But his thirteen-year-old got a terminal diagnosis and he started spending all his time off at Children's Medical Center. I remembered what it was like with Wyatt and I guess I felt sorry for Charles. His daughter passed away and his wife left him. He seemed all alone in the world. I thought he needed a friend. Hell, I needed a friend. I thought being pals was where it was all headed but then we were both lonely." She shrugged as more tears spilled out of her eyes. "One thing led to another. It all seemed harmless enough until I realized he was developing deeper feelings. I'm broken in that way. I can't go there with anyone."

She flashed her eyes at him as though she expected a reaction.

She wasn't going to get one, not one of judgment, anyway. He understood lonely and maybe that was the strong pull to her. They'd both experienced heartache and been let down by people. He could guess the rest of the story between her and Charles from there and the fact that it had ended badly.

He admired her courage. "From what I know about you so far, you're incredibly brave."

Leah was shaking her head.

"It's true." He figured he'd only heard the tip of the iceberg of her story, and here she was helping others find answers.

What questions kept her awake at night?

"I'm fine." She set down her coffee cup. "It's Jillian Mitchell's family that I'm worried about."

He felt a wall come up. Did she feel the need to protect herself from him?

It was smart of her. After hearing her story, his attraction had grown and he didn't mean the physical part. There was no question about the sexual current being stronger than anything he'd ever experienced. Her mind fascinated him, the way she thought.

It was easy to see that she was a caring person and he seriously doubted she would've pushed her own parents away if they'd made any real effort. She mentioned that she and her son saw her parents once a year. If Leah didn't want a relationship with them, she wouldn't even make that much effort. What she'd said about Dougherty lingered in his mind. Deacon didn't care what the man had been through—and the thought of losing a child or watching one die wasn't something he took lightly. That didn't give anyone a free pass to abuse others.

Charles Dougherty needed to stay in check. Deacon would keep an eye on the detective.

"It's not in your best interest to be seen with me." Deacon stood up to leave.

"I don't care what other people think," she said quickly. She stood and shrugged out of his jacket. She immediately shivered with the blast of cold air that came next as she handed it back to him.

"Wear it. It's big enough to give you easy access to your weapon but still keep you warm," he said. "I'm fine without it."

"Take your coat, Deacon." She shoved it toward him, and there was so much hurt and vulnerability in her eyes.

"Hell, I didn't mean to offend you." He grabbed the material being thrust into his chest with enough force to leave a mark.

"In case you don't know, I've been taking care of myself for a very long time and I don't need you or anyone else taking pity on me." Leah tossed the empty coffee cup in the nearby trash can.

"Need or want?" Seeing the vulnerability in

Leah's eyes shouldn't have made him want to kiss it away. Fireworks had been simmering between them from the first meeting, and despite the circumstances the flame had been lit. Fanning it would have been a mistake in the big picture but his in-the-moment mind argued for it.

"What's the difference?" She stood there in front of him, glaring at him, daring him to answer.

Leah Cordon was temptation in leggings and a sweatshirt.

Since she was so close and because her lips were too damn tempting, he asked, "What would you do if I kissed you right now?"

Chapter Eleven

Leah would kiss Deacon right back, even though she realized it wasn't the right call to make. Her judgment with men after Charles had her second-guessing her instincts. So she just stood there with her arms folded and a serious gaze fixed on Deacon.

"I'm not trying to frustrate you with my question." Deacon stood there, looking a little too kissable. Leah sighed sharply. She knew exactly what she wanted to do and that wasn't at all what she should. The irritating thought that coffee tasted better on his lips crept in.

"You don't really want to know my answer."

"Can I walk you home?" More of that Cowboy Code chivalry was shining through.

She motioned toward the butt of her weapon. "I have coverage."

Leah rubbed her cold arms.

"Good night," she said and then turned toward her place. Riley would be worried if Leah didn't get home soon. Leah had warned Riley that the killer was still at large. She'd told her to keep her guard up and that's exactly what Leah intended to do.

"Do you believe it's possible the killer changed tools?" Deacon asked.

She stopped but didn't turn. Walking away from him was proving to be so much more difficult than she had expected.

"No. It's too rare. Killers rarely change their MO. It becomes their calling card. In my mind, we're looking at two killers."

"Are you going to keep looking for him while you're on leave?" Deacon's voice was behind her now and it rumbled in her ear.

How easy would it be to lean back and feel his strong chest at her back? His muscular arms around her? His heated breath on her neck?

"Last night, I didn't sleep a wink thinking about this case. You want to have another cup of coffee? This one's cold," he asked.

Leah stood there, debating her next actions. She was at a crossroads.

"I live at six-twenty-three Maple Ave. My son's down for the count tonight. Wait fifteen minutes, park across the street and I'll have a fresh pot on." She didn't turn around. She didn't wait for his answer. She wasn't the least bit tired and knew full well that she'd end up staring up at the ceiling if she tried to go to bed when she got home.

Leah jogged toward her house, relieved that she could hear Deacon's footsteps not more than ten feet behind her. His presence was comforting.

He stood in front of the O'Malleys' place three houses down and across the street, waiting for her to get safely inside her house before he disappeared down the same path as before.

Her heart squeezed as he took off running.

Riley popped up off the couch. Her silver laptop closed and clutched against her chest like a school book. "I was just about to text to see if you were okay."

"Met up with someone on the trail and we ended up talking for a bit." It was true.

Riley nodded and smiled. "I have another test, so the quiet was much appreciated. Connor hasn't made a peep in the last twenty minutes. I checked on him anyway. It's so weird about the Mitchell case. I mean, I know this guy isn't after little kids but it all makes me nervous. It's all so disturbing. You know?"

Leah did know. There were many aspects of her job that sometimes kept her awake at night, wondering why people did certain things to each other. "It's good to be vigilant but that doesn't mean we stop living. We just make sure we're prepared."

Riley patted the bottle of Mace clipped to her shoulder bag. "I'm ready."

"Did you sign up for the jujitsu class at the rec?" Leah would always make sure those around her knew how to defend themselves should the situation arise.

"It was full. Guess people want to be extra prepared. Good timing if you ask me," Riley said.

"Stay on it so you can register next time. I can't have you going off to college without taking some kind of defense lessons." If Leah had a daughter, she would tell her the same things she would be telling her son his senior year of high school.

"Okay. I will. First things first, I have a trig test tomorrow and I'm so not ready." Riley was only dramatic when it came to schoolwork, and she always sandbagged when it came to grades.

"You'll do great." Leah didn't remind Riley that she'd said the same thing about the last three tests she'd taken. All of which she'd broken the curve on.

"I doubt it but there's not much I can do now." She bit back a yawn. "Sleep calls and I can't stay up much longer."

"See you tomorrow night? Same time?" Leah

walked Riley to the back door and then stood in the frame for a few more seconds, listening for any signs. The creepy feeling of eyes on her pricked the hairs on her neck. She stepped outside and through the back gate, scanning the alley for signs of movement. A gust of wind nearly made her jump when it rattled a patch of dead leaves.

What would she be jumping at next? Stray cats? Speaking of which, she hadn't seen her favorite alley predator in a couple of days now. Pickles didn't belong to Leah and she couldn't figure for the life of her why Connor had come up with that name, but the little tabby normally stopped by in the morning and evenings and Leah hadn't seen her around.

Almost the minute after Riley disappeared, Deacon rounded the drive. The noise scared Leah because she hadn't heard a thing until he was within striking distance.

"Come in." She took a deep breath to calm her racing pulse—racing for a reason other than being startled.

DEACON FOLLOWED LEAH into her kitchen. "After tonight, we can't be seen together."

"I was just thinking the same thing."

The admission caught him off guard. Was it

wrong that he wanted her to be thinking about something else?

"You need to focus on keeping your name clear," she said.

"And you could lose your career." Leah was a single mother and he couldn't afford to let that happen to her. He'd witnessed his brother Mitch handling newborn twins when his wife went missing three and a half years ago. Even with plenty of financial resources, bringing them up alone had been difficult. Plus, Mitch had his brothers and sister along with their cousins, Amy and Zach McWilliams.

Leah produced two full mugs of coffee. "No matter what else happens, I'd like to stay in touch. Keep each other informed of the other's progress. I realize I'll get some details through formal chains, but I have a feeling you won't tell your cousin anything before you're ready."

"As long as information flows both ways, I have no problem with that." Deacon took a sip of coffee. The dark roast burned in the best possible way. "We can start with what kind of person would do this?"

"I'm looking at my case and yours as two separate perps." She leaned her slender hip against the counter and gripped her coffee mug with two hands.

"As am I."

A noise sounded in the alley right outside the back door and Leah flinched for a split second before hopping into action. She turned off the light and dropped down low and away from the window, palming her holstered weapon.

With stealth and grace, she moved to the door.

More of the same sounds came but he was pretty sure he recognized a cat scratching on a door when he heard it. He didn't have to be brought up on a ranch to know that sound. Although, it probably didn't hurt that he'd spent his entire childhood and most of his adult life around animals.

Before he could stop Leah, she'd opened the door and her gun was pointing toward the culprit. A cat.

"Pickles." She holstered her weapon and then picked up the little tabby.

"That's an interesting name." Deacon thought there'd never been a stranger name for a tabby.

"Connor's idea."

"How old is your son again?" Deacon hoped the little guy was young. And then he remembered about the time she said the number, three. "Never mind. After being around my niece and nephew, I understand. Nothing has to make sense."

She nuzzled the furry critter and Deacon couldn't help but wish it were him and not that cat up close and personal with Leah. Those were more thoughts that had no business in their new arrangement—one he fully intended to honor.

Most of the people he knew who worked in law enforcement had a story, a reason they decided to wear a badge and lock up bad guys. They all started with wanting to help but came from many backgrounds and experiences.

Case in point, one of his cousin Zach's deputies who grew up in a rural area had always looked up to the local sheriff. The sheriff took Herman Long on a ride along in order to keep him out of trouble, Long had said. But then on a routine traffic stop, the guy witnessed the sheriff being shot. The car sped off and Long was too panicked to get the license plate or a description. This was obviously before the sophisticated computer systems that linked data and made it available to anyone with a few keystrokes. It was before dashboard cameras. Long had said that right then and there he'd decided to become a law enforcement officer. And he had done just that.

What Deacon wanted to know was what had happened to make a rich girl from The Heights want to grow up to work in law enforcement. "What made you decide to do this job?"

"Huh?" Leah seemed caught off guard at

the question. She was crouched down, petting the tabby.

"Why chase bad guys? What's the appeal?"

She reclaimed her coffee mug and gripped it with both hands again. And then she looked him in the eyes. "Because I don't want to be afraid of one ever again."

Damn. What was Deacon supposed to do with that?

"You grew up in one of the safest neighborhoods." She'd briefly told him about her best friend being killed. His curiosity about the case was getting the best of him. But, honestly, he wanted to know more about her.

She stood there and it seemed like she was drawing up the courage to speak. It hit him that her story must be difficult to talk about and he didn't want to be the jerk pushing her to do something she didn't want to.

"I apologize. You don't have to talk about the past," he said.

"I never talk about it," she said low and almost under her breath. "I never talk about what really happened to *her.*"

Leah motioned toward the table and chairs in the small kitchen.

He followed her and took the seat opposite hers. Her place was the kind of spot he could envision kicking his boots off and staying a little while. He had no plans to do that but the idea of it wasn't awful.

"We were best friends," she began.

"Is this the friend you mentioned from high school?" he asked.

"Yes," was all she said. She looked like she needed a minute to pull herself together.

He remembered that she'd said her friend had died but the full picture was beginning to emerge. One that confirmed her friend was murdered.

"Millie and I weren't supposed to go out that night but we decided to anyway. It was April. We had spring fever. It was our junior year. High school was intense and the stress of upcoming finals was starting to get to us. We wanted to blow off steam and one of our classmates was having a party across town. I was supposed to meet up with her but I fell asleep instead." The contents of her coffee cup became intensely interesting right about then. "I'd been wrapped up in studying all night and thought I could just close my eyes for a few minutes."

Deacon reached out to one of her hands. To his surprise, she grabbed onto his with a glance at him before returning her gaze to the mug.

Her hand seemed so small in comparison to his. Her creamy skin was soft. Long hours on the ranch had calloused his.

"They found her body two weeks later and I went down to the morgue with her parents to ID her." Leah sat there for a long moment and he waited for her to speak again. "So, my story is that my best friend was killed because I fell asleep. No one ever found her killer or could explain what had happened to her beyond her being dead. My parents gave me a summer to get over it and then expected me to jump right into senior year..."

"But you couldn't because you carried around too much guilt," he finished the sentence for her.

"I wanted to know what happened to her. They said the details weren't important because they wouldn't bring her back but that getting into a good college was. They told me to look to my future, which was a way of saying that she was in the past. I mean, it had barely been four months and the killer was still on the loose, preying on other girls and my parents were worried that my SAT score wouldn't be good enough to follow in my mother's footsteps and get into Brown University." Deacon felt her grip tighten on his hand but he didn't flinch.

"It mattered to you." He didn't dare let go.

"What they didn't—don't—understand is that I couldn't walk away because I never got answers. If I'd known what had happened to her, it would've made a difference in my life. I could've put that chapter behind me. That's why I do what I do. It's the reason that I have to work for other people."

He stopped short of responding that she gave to others what she never got for herself.

"Have you looked at the case file?" Her fingers relaxed against his.

"Dozens of times. Knowing what I know now, I think it's safe to say the man who killed Millie ended up in prison for another crime." She scraped her teeth across her bottom lip. He'd noticed the move before when she'd spoken about her friend.

"What about her family?"

"I haven't spoken to them in years," she admitted.

Did she have a case of survivor's guilt?

Yeah, he could relate to wishing he were the one who was dead.

Chapter Twelve

The next time Deacon glanced at the clock it was five o'clock in the morning. He should've been at work on the ranch half an hour ago if he hadn't fallen asleep. Time seemed to disappear when he was with Leah.

"It's late." He paused for a beat. "Or early, depending on your disposition."

Leah's cell buzzed from where it sat on the counter.

She shot a concerned look at him before hopping up, breaking the link with their fingers.

"It's Dougherty." Was it wrong that Deacon liked that she used the man's last name? Referring to him by his first would imply a lot more intimacy. Deacon had no right to be jealous in any case, even though his heart argued the opposite.

She answered the call. "It's no big deal. I'm already awake." Dougherty must've started right in, skipping pleasantries. It was another thing that Deacon liked. Again, less intimate. "No reason. Couldn't sleep is all."

Deacon understood why she couldn't tell Dougherty the situation. Hell, Deacon was the one who'd insisted the two of them not be seen together. So it was ridiculous that his heart fisted when she said the words out loud. Deacon needed to get a grip. It was most likely because he'd just spoken more words to her than he had to anyone in the past year in one night. Leah was easy to talk to. There was so much vulnerability lurking behind the steel facade she'd erected. There was something pure and honest about her reactions to the world that was unexpected for someone who spent most of her day chasing down the worst of humanity.

And, although Deacon didn't believe in love at first sight—no matter how quick and unexpected the lightning bolt that had zapped him at his initial encounter with the espresso-haired beauty— he did believe that an instant connection was possible. That something down deep could be a magnet to someone else. He'd never experienced it until now, though. Even his connection with Jackie hadn't come this easily straight out of the gate.

Thinking of her brought back a flood of memories he couldn't afford. Thinking about the bond they'd shared—one he never thought was possible again—caused all his defenses to engage.

Deacon had loved Jackie. Losing her, losing her child, who hadn't been his but he couldn't have loved more anyway, was a gut punch. He stood, suddenly needing fresh air.

Leah covered the mouthpiece of the phone. "What's wrong?"

He waved her off and stepped outside. Hearing about the phone call could wait until he could breathe again.

Outside, the sun wouldn't be up for another couple of hours and it was pitch-black. The wind was a steady force, whipping around his face. There was air all around but his lungs still clawed for it, couldn't seem to take any in.

He doubled over, fisted his right hand and then gave his chest a quick pound. Jump-starting his breathing didn't work. Deacon stood again to his full height of six feet four inches. He jumped up and down a few times, trying to stimulate his nervous system to start working again. It felt like everything inside him was shutting down.

All he could do was fight against the current sweeping him under and tossing him out to sea.

Just as he was taking in a lung full of air for what felt like the first time, Leah appeared at the doorway. She wore an expression that was a mix of concern and grief.

"Another body was found," she said. "A diver pulled a female victim who is missing a foot out of the Trinity River. There's been no ID, so the victim is going on the Jane Doe list until we can positively identify her." Deacon didn't want to think about the family who would be missing a wife, mother, daughter only to discover she'd been brutally murdered. His blood heated. "The victim has the same color of hair as Jillian Mitchell. The woman is also around her height and age."

"Which means someone is targeting a specific kind of woman. How far away from Porter's Bend did this happen?" He wanted to know just how close to home this went. The Trinity River itself was something close to seven hundred miles long or greater he'd read a few years back in connection to an unrelated news story.

A noise behind Leah caused her to whirl around.

"Hey, little man." She dropped down to crouching position and Deacon saw little arms wrap around her neck.

Time and space seemed to stop as a flash of Jackie with her little girl in a similar position stamped his thoughts. The sudden urge to get the hell out of there slammed into him. He took off jogging in the direction of his vehicle and had to remind himself to breathe. His chest felt like it was about to detonate.

It was an odd feeling because he'd been around mothers and babies from his brothers' families and had never experienced any blow-back from it. What was different about Leah and her son that had Deacon turning tail faster than he could remind himself that this wasn't the same situation? This wasn't Jackie and Emery.

Repeating the statement half a dozen times couldn't deaden the effect the sight had had on him.

A sudden burst of rage caused him to lash out against a tree. He bare-knuckle punched it. Feelings he'd stuffed so deep he thought they'd never surface again shot through him. Anger? Check. Grief? Check. Helplessness? Check.

White-hot anger exploded in another round of self-hate. Why couldn't he have saved them? Why did this all seem so familiar? Nothing about the two women—Leah and Jackie—was the same other than both being single mothers. A thought struck like a bus on the freeway.

Those two women who were murdered looked similar to Leah. An irrational fear gripped him that she could be next. Could he survive if he were to lose another woman he cared about?

LEAH HELD ON TO her little boy after locking the door behind her. Deacon had taken off out of the blue and she racked her brain, trying to figure out what she'd said or done to cause him to do that.

"You're up early." She hugged Connor a little tighter this morning and especially after the news of the second body that had turned up. Finding answers might have been what drove her to be one of the best detectives at Fort Worth PD but holding this little guy kept her sane. Everything about her toddler reminded her there was still innocence and beauty in the world.

Thinking about his father and her relationship with him, she could admit that her parents might've been right. She may have married him in an act of rebellion after she brought him home to get their opinion and they balked. The things they'd said to her after dinner that night might've been what had driven her straight into his arms. Looking back, she realized that she hadn't loved him—or anyone—in that all-consuming feeling that she'd heard people could have for each other. Leah had been content with Wyatt. She'd cared for him deeply and he'd been the calm in a storm. Had she gotten into the relationship because he was safe? Because there'd be no losing her heart? No pain if it had ended?

The last part couldn't be true because she'd experienced real hurt when Wyatt had died. Crawl-in-bed-for-days pain. There'd been so much going on in her mind back then with Connor on the way and her husband suddenly gone. And then her parents had seemed almost relieved to hear that Wyatt had had a terminal diagnosis. That that would somehow get him out of the picture and them off the hook.

When she'd accused them of that very thing days before his funeral, they'd denied it and asked how cruel she thought they were. And that had almost gotten her thinking that they really did care, until they heard about the pregnancy and threatened to cut her out of their lives if she didn't *take care of it*.

A renewed anger struck at the memory of it. But she didn't want her boy's first interaction with her in the morning to be full of it.

Leah plastered on a smile, thinking about the old fake-it-till-you-make-it phrase. "How about pancakes this morning, buddy?"

Connor's eyes lit up at that as he hugged her shoulder and his favorite blanket. He worked the silk material around the edges between his finger and thumb. It was adorable the way he held onto that blue blanket like it was worth more than gold. He looked like her in almost every way except he had his father's eyes.

The last couple of days had hit a high peak on the emotional scale. Talking to Deacon and opening up about so much of her past had released a surprising amount of pent-up feelings.

Seeing her son's face reminded her why she got out of bed every morning to face another day. Deacon had her thinking about things like having a normal family. She quickly told herself not with him, but the idea in general didn't make her tense up. Could she someday down the road think about opening her heart to someone?

THIRTY-TWO HOURS went by before Leah heard from Deacon again. His text said that he was nearby and wanted to see if she was awake so they could talk.

A knock at the back door shouldn't have caught her off guard, considering she knew Deacon was on his way. She jumped despite herself. Answering the door, seeing him shouldn't have made her stomach perform a gymnastic routine. It did.

"I already put on a pot of coffee." She tried to hide the flush in her cheeks and most likely failed miserably.

He greeted her and then reclaimed his same seat from the other night.

"Everything okay at the ranch?" There were dark circles underneath his eyes and scruff on his chin like he hadn't shaved in a couple of days.

"There haven't been any new injured heifers since I last saw you. We've been keeping security tight and taking extra shifts patrolling." That must account for the look of no sleep. "But that's not why I'm here. We didn't get a chance to finish our conversation the other night."

"That's what you said in your text." Leah handed him a cup of fresh brew. He took it and thanked her. Their fingers brushed and she ignored the electricity causing hers to tingle and pulse. She sat down across the table from him and did her level best to avoid prolonged eye contact.

"Is what the media printed about the second murder true?" he asked.

"Yes. It was her right foot and cut clean off." Revisiting the details sent a chill racing down Leah's back.

"Just like Jillian Mitchell." Deacon white-knuckled his coffee mug.

She nodded confirmation.

"Is there a positive ID on the victim?" He took a sip of coffee.

It was colder outside than it had been all week, which was saying a lot. She'd nearly frozen on her jog.

"Delaney Richards. She was twenty-nine years old." That and the other information she was about to share had been kept out of the news. "She has a similar description to Jillian

Mitchell, and with the same MO we have every reason to believe the cases are linked."

"Is Detective Dougherty keeping you in the loop?" He didn't look up at her when he asked so she couldn't read his eyes.

"More or less." She shrugged. "He tells me some information and the rest I'm picking up from colleagues."

"How long had she been in the river before they found her?" he asked.

"Less than twelve hours." Leah sipped her coffee.

"We were on that same trail, on the same night," he said.

"I know." Could they have stopped it?

"I didn't hear anything." His voice was so low when he said it that she almost didn't hear him.

"If we'd known, we would've prevented it. We were far enough away that even if she screamed, which she may not have, we wouldn't have heard. The victims might know this guy personally. Dougherty is working on finding a link but there's nothing on the surface. He still says Elijah Henry is guilty, although there's no evidence connecting him to the crime. He'd been released hours before it had happened and, again, he doesn't have much of an alibi." Deacon clearly didn't agree. Blaming himself for not being able to stop the crime wouldn't do any good. Leah was an expert at that and it never changed the outcome.

"What time does that put her at the scene? She could've shown up after we left." His reasoning wasn't off base and was the first thing Leah's mind snapped to.

"It's only a guess. Forensics is still evaluating—"

"What does Rex think?" He pinned her with his stare.

She slid her left hand under her leg. "Based on what he says, the times match up."

"So every jogger or walker on the Trinity River Trail who's out at night is at risk?" He placed his flat palm on the table. "That really narrows it down."

"He could strike anywhere. We can't let our guard down just because he's hit twice in the same spot. We don't know enough about his psychology to predict his next move." She took a sip of coffee. "That being said, the chief is doubling up patrols along the path. He's offering overtime pay for officers willing to work extra hours."

"I'm guessing that with all of these officers being positioned on the trail—"

Leah was already nodding her head before he finished his sentence.

He tapped his fingers on the table. "Makes you think other areas of the city are vulnerable."

"Dougherty has had tunnel vision all along on this case," she said. "I don't want to make the same mistakes."

"He released Elijah Henry. My family's lawyer is working the case," Deacon pointed out.

"Only to turn around and try to bring him back in." She sighed. "And now Henry has disappeared."

"As in you can't find him or something might've happened to him?" Deacon seemed to be chewing on that thought for a minute.

"I'm not sure. I've asked my colleagues and informants to let me know if they see him. Of course, they'll have to bring him into the station for questioning now that Dougherty put out a Be-On-The-Look-Out, BOLO. Once Dougherty locks on to someone or something, he doesn't easily change his mind."

Deacon took another sip of coffee. "Dougherty's history with the department has been solid. The chief most likely won't take him off the case."

"I go back in three days. It'll be easier for me to get information once I'm back on the streets. Cops talk. T-Rex, you already met him, he talks. Jailers talk. I come into contact with these men and women every day through the course of my job. No one will think anything if I ask about the case. It's high profile so everyone's ready to throw out a theory." She checked the clock. They'd been talking for a solid hour.

"The victims both had dark hair and dark eyes." Deacon was studying her.

"So do thousands of other women who live in Fort Worth," she stated. "There were no similarities in jobs or friends. There's no family connection. They don't live on the same side of town. One of the victims had a dog. The other couldn't keep a fish alive, according to her boyfriend. Jillian Mitchell was married and thinking about starting a family. Delaney Richards was single and working toward a promotion at the hospital where she worked in the patient intake department. Jillian Mitchell hasn't been anywhere near a hospital in the last ten years. Not so much as an X-ray."

"Sounds like this guy has a thing for brown-haired, brown-eyed joggers," Deacon pointed out. He studied her, taking in the features he'd just described.

"Right. Just like me."

He nodded and his lips thinned.

Before Leah realized, she'd been talking to Deacon all night. Sun peeked through the kitchen curtains. Noise from the other room startled her until she heard Connor's soft cry.

"That's my cue." Leah set her coffee cup down and stood. "I'll be right back."

She saw an emotion flicker behind Deacon's eyes that she couldn't quite pinpoint. And then he nodded.

Leah started down the hall. "Coming, sweet boy."

Connor was in the early waking stage. He rubbed his eyes as she kneeled next to his big boy bed. "Good morning."

His sleepy yawn tugged at her heart. No matter how tough the past three years had been, she didn't regret having her son for a second. Her relationship with Wyatt might not have been *love–love*, but she'd genuinely cared about her husband as much as she could allow herself to invest emotionally in anyone. She couldn't regret the relationship, not when it had produced their son. She shoved the thought down deep and picked up her waking angel.

"Did you have a good sleep?" she asked quietly in his ear.

"Uh-huh." Connor's vocabulary had exploded in the past year and a half but one would never know that this early in the morning. This time was reserved for sleepy grunts. For a kid who woke up consistently at the crack of dawn, he didn't *do* mornings very well.

Leah hugged her son close.

"Mama, waffles?" Connor asked.

"Yes to waffles," she said. "I have a friend over and we can see if he wants waffles, too."

In all the time she'd dated Charles Dougherty, she kept him away from her home. Dating life and home life seemed like a natural separation, so it surprised her when she realized that she wanted Connor to meet Deacon. It was probably just because Deacon was a good male role model and she was always on the lookout for those since Connor had lost his father.

She stopped off at the bathroom, which was always the first pit stop for her son after first waking. And then she picked up Connor, kissed him on the forehead and walked toward the kitchen.

There was no one sitting at the kitchen table.

Chapter Thirteen

Deacon had called twice and Leah hadn't picked up either time. She was still confused by his actions—actions that had her believing he didn't want anything to do with her child.

The day was a blur of preschool drop-off and pick-up, grocery shopping and cleaning. By the time dinner rolled around, Leah was certain that being home with her son all day was more work than her full-time job. Both were important and she needed the money so there was no choice about working. But her fantasy that being a stay-at-home mom would somehow be easier was obliterated. Wasn't there some kind of network that would make the job manageable and less isolating?

Even though conversation with Connor was pretty much numbers and alphabet rehearsals, she felt more fulfilled at the end of day, which struck her as weird. She'd always believed that she worked in order to find that feeling. By the time Riley arrived, Leah was ready to bounce off the walls. She needed her exercise time now more than ever.

"How was school today?" Leah asked, mostly just making conversation as she put on her running shoes.

"Best day ever." Riley beamed.

Leah took a closer look. Her babysitter practically glowed. "What's that smile all about? You're sick of school, remember?"

"Do you remember me talking about Drew?" Riley asked sheepishly.

"Football team Drew?" Leah asked. "Quarterback Drew? The kid who annoyed the heck out of you in pre-calc?"

"He's not so bad," Riley defended.

Uh-oh.

"Anything that gets you excited about going to school again isn't going to bother me," Leah said. Riley had the worst case of senioritis. "What about him?"

"He talked to me today."

Well, someone sound the bell tower.

"And?"

"That's it." Riley shrugged. "He told me about a party he might be going to this weekend. He said it would be cool if I showed up."

"I don't mean to play the *old lady card* here but that doesn't exactly sound like he asked you out on a date." Leah knew that some of the shier guys had a difficult time coming up with the right words and fear of rejection had them keeping conversation general. But she wished he'd given a clearer signal.

Was she still talking about Riley?

"He probably just wants to hang out first. You know, see if we get along before he makes it official." Riley tried so hard to sound like she didn't care.

"Well, kiddo, that sounds like a good plan to me. I mean, you may not find that the two of you have much in common after being around each other outside of school." Leah had a hard time believing a quarterback of a good high school football team could be shy, but she'd seen more shocking things than that. She imagined he had young girls lining up to date him. Leah had had a terrible experience and her defenses were showing. Riley was a beautiful young woman with brains to spare. Now that she really thought about it, why wouldn't he want to date her? Leah guessed she saw Riley with someone who spent more time with his nose in a book than outside on a playing field. But, hey, if this guy made her happy, good for her.

"It's kind of weird because I don't believe in, like, love at first sight. But there was just this instant *boom* in my head the first time we made eye contact. I was standing at my locker talking to Valerie and when I shut the door and turned around, there he was talking to one of his teammates." She made a dramatic gesture with her hands. "This doesn't sound like me at all, I know, but it's all true."

Seeing the openness in Riley's smile, the innocence in her eyes made Leah think she was too cynical. "And he's as smart as you?"

"He's in the running for valedictorian," Riley practically exclaimed.

Wow. To be young and have such an overwhelming crush. Leah couldn't remember the last time… Well, there was Brock Garrison her freshman year. He'd given her all those giddy, giggly feelings. He'd been a lifeguard at the pool by the high school. He was a junior when she was a freshman and he barely looked her way, except that one time in the hallway before Christmas break. She'd stayed after for English tutoring and the school seemed almost empty by the time tutoring was over. Leah sat on the front steps, waiting. And then out of those same doors walked Brock. He lifted weights but he wasn't big like some of the football players. He was more toned than bulky. He stopped and asked to sit next to her. Leah could hardly believe it. Her cheeks heated and she was embarrassingly tongue-tied but he was smooth.

The two chatted easily, and as her mother pulled up he asked for her phone number. A few days later, he called and asked her out for the coming Saturday.

The date was short-lived. He'd taken her to a party where she sat awkwardly because none of her circle of friends was there. All the kids were older. She watched as he popped open a beer. She didn't want to get in the car with him after he started drinking and he seemed more into his buddies than he was into her, so she slipped out the back door, figuring she could walk home.

The jock who'd followed her had other ideas. Rad Clemens was a star running back. He was already being scouted by colleges in his junior year. He was also full of himself sober and worse when he'd been drinking.

Leah had figured out what was going on a few seconds too late to turn around. Music thumped from the party and no one would hear her if she screamed. A fact that Rad seemed keenly aware of, too. She'd picked up the pace, figuring that she could probably outrun him in his drunken state. He'd been surprisingly fast. His vise-like grip around her arm stopped her cold in her tracks.

She'd tried to jerk free but his fist was clamped. He'd asked her where she thought she was going. He'd spun her around like she weighed nothing and laughed at the sheer look of terror that had to have been on her face.

Biting, kicking and screaming had saved her that night. A neighbor heard the racket and came out of his house to yell at them. When he saw what was happening, he threatened to call the police if Rad didn't let her go.

After Rad took off running back to the party, he'd told Brock that she'd come on to him. Brock had left her a nasty message on her answering machine. There was no point arguing her case the next day, either. He believed Rad.

Leah shook off the recollection and finished tying her shoe. "Be careful. Stick with a friend and don't walk home alone."

Of course, that was true about people in general but she tried to keep her warnings to a minimum.

"I'm not crazy. I mean, I'm taking it slow. You know, chill." Riley was trying too hard to convince Leah. So Leah smiled.

Chill?

"Of course you are." Leah had to stifle a laugh. Kids went through some interesting changes in high school. Oh, to be seventeen again. There was so much Leah would have done differently.

"Have a great run." Riley was clearly changing the subject.

"I might be later than usual tonight. I need this

today." Taking her new respect for stay-at-home moms with her, Leah hoped she could exercise herself out of the funk she'd been in most of the day. Her shackles were still rankled over Deacon's disappearing act.

It took a good twenty minutes after she warmed up to hit her running stride. Rounding the corner and seeing Deacon was the emotional equivalent of slamming into a brick wall at eighty miles an hour.

"What are you doing here?"

"APOLOGIZING FOR THE WAY I left things this morning." Deacon had bolted out in a hurry and then had thought about her the entire day. He'd had a difficult time thinking about anything *but* her.

She stood there, chest heaving and arms folded but saying nothing.

"I'm not *that* guy—"

"You mean the one who scribbles a note on a scrap piece of paper and sneaks out the door?" Yeah, she had a right to be angry about that.

"It didn't seem right for your son to wake up to a stranger in the house." That was true. It wasn't the entire reason he'd bolted. How could he explain that seeing her holding her child might just shock him back to a time when he'd fallen for another single mother? Both were dead now and he'd sworn off caring for anyone else in the same situation. Losing two of the people he'd cared about most had nearly done him in. His heart had an auto-shutoff valve engaged now to protect him from ever experiencing that level of pain again.

"I don't make a habit of telling people my life story. I guess I figured you wrong." Leah studied him. In her line of work, she'd have a good idea if someone were telling the truth. He was losing and if he wanted to spend any more time around her—and he did—he was going to have to give her more to go on.

"In my past, I dated a woman with a child." He hoped like hell she could understand.

Leah's toe was tapping out a staccato rhythm on the pavement.

"A little girl, Emery, and she had a hard time meeting new people." Leah examined him like she was looking right through him. Did she see beneath the layers of metal into the core of him? Deacon felt exposed talking about his past. He didn't *go there* with anyone, either.

"I get that," she said. "Is that really the reason?"

She was perceptive. Smart. Beautiful.

"It's part of it." Deacon wasn't a liar. "The other side of the coin has to do with me."

"You don't like kids?" Her question came out rushed and there was at least a hint of disappointment in her tone. She quickly covered it by squaring her shoulders.

"That's not the problem." He didn't want to tell her that his heart couldn't allow him to get attached to another woman and her child.

"Then what is?" Her gaze narrowed and her lips thinned. She was getting impatient and, hell, he couldn't blame her. If the shoe were on the other foot, he wouldn't like what he was hearing, either.

"It's me. Okay? I can't get close to another kid and…"

"I get it." She held up her hand. "She broke up with you and you lost two people and that's awful for anyone. But meeting my son—"

"She didn't break up with me…" He let his voice trail off because he couldn't say it out loud. Not even now.

Catching her gaze, her mouth formed an *Oh*.

It looked like the wind had been knocked out of her. "I'm so sorry for your loss, Deacon. I truly am."

Those words shouldn't have soothed him in the way that they did.

She said other things like, "That's not fair." And it wasn't. Feeling sorry for himself, licking his wounds like he'd been doing for the past year didn't change anything, wouldn't bring Jackie and Emery back. No amount of pounding his fists into a wall could do that.

His hands fisted at his sides thinking about it, but Leah took a couple of steps toward him, closing the distance. He could see her breath in the cold night air as she said other words of comfort. And then she clutched his jacket and tugged him toward her. Deacon took in a deep breath, steadying himself as the world stopped spinning for the first time in twelve long months.

He couldn't be sure how long they stood there. It was like time had stopped and the world shrank to only the two of them. He brought his hands up to her neck and pressed his forehead to hers, not wanting to think about how good she smelled when they were toe-to-toe or how much he liked the taste of coffee so much better on her lips.

Before he did something stupid, like kiss her again, he took her hands in his and dropped them down to her sides. "You want to run? I'd like to be your shadow. All I could think about today was you being safe."

"I'm a trained officer of the law. I can handle most situations." There was no rebuttal in her eyes. "But I'm also a mother and need to make it home to my son every night. So I won't ask you not to follow me. I'll be grateful for any extra set of eyes I can get."

After standing there a few more seconds, she replaced an earbud and jogged away from him.

Deacon kept pace about fifteen feet behind Leah. They'd been running—and she was a solid runner—for almost half an hour when she stopped as a man came into view. Charles Dougherty in all black jogging gear was more than a little creepy.

"What are you doing here, Charles? You're not a runner." Deacon kept a distance but made sure the detective could see him clearly.

Dougherty's gaze bounced from Leah to Deacon and back. His eyebrows were slashes and his cheeks fire red.

"I have a killer on this trail. Why are you still out here?" He glared at Leah.

"Last time I checked, this was a free country, Charles. And this is *my* trail. You know that." Her voice was chillier than the air outside.

"We need to talk in private," he demanded. There he went with that line again.

"That's not going to happen, Charles."

"I have another dead body because you went to the chief and filled his head with a bunch of nonsense about Henry not being my guy." Charles took a threatening step toward her. His hands fisted at his sides.

"Hey, there. Calm down. There's no reason we can't discuss this like rational adults." Deacon needed to let Charles know that his behavior was unacceptable. And if the rational adults path didn't work, Charles was going to come to understand that Deacon would take him on man-to-man. Either way, the detective wasn't about to lay a hand on Leah.

Leah poked her index finger in Dougherty's chest. "You take another step or raise your fist at me and I will go to the chief. Your badge will hang over my fireplace mantel."

Deacon almost chuckled. So much for coming to the aid of a lady when that female happened to be a cop and could take care of herself. Even so, Dougherty had an unfair size advantage and—according to Deacon—an anger management problem that needed to be addressed. Deacon remembered the story about the detective's daughter and wife, and that caused him to soften his stance a little.

"You need to know that you're playing with fire," Dougherty shot back. He took a step in the opposite direction of Leah.

"There's no need to threaten me, Charles—"

"Is the prospect of losing your job not important enough for you to keep away from *him*?" Dougherty motioned toward Deacon.

The detective needed to get a grip. "If you want to discuss the case with her, fine. But don't speak down to her like that again. It's her business who she talks to and just because we happened to run into each other on the same trail doesn't mean we came here together."

They hadn't. Deacon had no problem pointing out the truth.

"Oh, yeah? What about your overnight visits to her house?" Dougherty shot back.

Deacon thought about planting a fist on Dougherty's jaw. Leah pushed in between them as though she read his mind.

Fire shot through Dougherty's glare.

"Say what you want about anyone else, but when it comes to me and Leah, you'd be advised to mind your own business." Leah's palm was firmly planted on Deacon's chest. He had no intention of losing control or charging the detective but Dougherty needed to know he'd crossed the line.

"Is that what you want?" Dougherty wagged a finger at Deacon.

Leah seemed to realize that Deacon wasn't a charging bull and she stepped aside. Dougherty took advantage and snapped a kick off at Deacon, nailing him in the stomach. Deacon doubled over as the heel of Dougherty's boot slammed into his ribs and then his fist connected with Deacon's eye.

Deacon instantly reacted with an uppercut that connected with Dougherty's nose. Blood splattered and Deacon thought for a split second that he might've just broken the detective's nose.

The man took a couple of steps back and shook his head like a wet dog. "That's a mistake you'll regret."

Leah was in between them again, playing referee, when Dougherty shoved her shoulder.

"Hey—" Leah couldn't finish her statement without Dougherty knocking her back a step.

"I'll have your badge over your boyfriend striking an officer of the law," Dougherty said to Leah. There was a lot of venom in his tone, which also told Deacon loud and clear that the man hadn't gotten over her.

"Go ahead. I'll have yours after I meet with the mayor. You'll both be unemployed. Is that what you want?" Deacon threatened. He'd never used his family name to back someone down before but Dougherty needed a slap of reality.

"You're about to see how bad life can get," Dougherty said to Leah as he stumbled away.

Chapter Fourteen

"Thank goodness, he's gone," Leah said to Deacon. "Are you all right?"

"He's been watching your house." Deacon's tone told her the situation hadn't defused yet.

"Come back to my place." She glanced around. She didn't want to leave things like this and she wanted to talk to him before he made that call to the mayor. "I don't like talking out here in the open and I'm cold."

Deacon took off his jacket and placed it around her shoulders.

"Thanks but now you'll freeze," she said.

"I'm fine." Deacon put his arm around her and she instantly warmed. "Someone needs to warn the chief about the detective's attitude. His breath smelled like alcohol. He's snooping in places he has no business and that'll get him hurt."

"I know he seems a little crazy right now but we take care of our own." She pulled out her phone and texted Keeve to make sure Dougherty didn't end up driving or going home alone to stew.

"Will you see me home?" She wanted to finish their conversation from earlier.

Deacon didn't immediately agree. "I'm not so sure that's a good idea. If he's watching your house, it could mean trouble for you. Your chief already warned you to make sure your priorities were aligned."

"Are you really afraid I'm going to lose my job? Is that really what's making you hesitate?" She wanted to know the truth because she was falling down that slippery slope of caring about Deacon Kent.

"If you do, I'll feel responsible," he admitted.

"But that's not the same."

"No. It isn't." He issued a sharp sigh and she thought for a split second that he was about to open up about what was wrong. But then he clamped his mouth shut and they were back at square one.

"You have connections. You could make a phone call and have both my chief and Charles jumping through hoops." She'd never witnessed Deacon threaten to throw his family's weight around, but she'd seen a healthy respect for the Kent name in the chief's eyes during their conversation last week.

"That's true." He stood there for a long moment. "I like you, Leah. More than I should. I'm starting to care about what happens to you and I don't want to."

If she hadn't known about his background, those words would've cut her to the quick.

"You're worried about me. Right?" she asked.

"Yes." He issued another sharp sigh.

"Then, see me home. I always let Riley out the back door. You can wait at the front," she said.

"And if Dougherty is watching?"

"So be it. I can't live my life based on what someone else thinks, Deacon. You know about what happened to me in my past and I think that's why you came here tonight. You of all people with your independent streak would realize how important it is to me not to let someone else control my actions. Because the man who took away my friend in high school sure as hell did. I was afraid of my own shadow for far too long after that experience. And no one gets to do that to me again." His thumb moved in circles on her shoulder, calming her more than she knew better than to allow. She felt safe with Deacon and that feeling was foreign at best, because even though she wore a badge and a gun to work every single day, she still felt vulnerable underneath all the external armor and internal walls she'd erected to keep people out. She told herself that it was good, that it kept her vigilant and probably saved her life. Being with Deacon gave her something no counselor could—peace of mind. Granted, they couldn't kiss again. That was a given. Her feelings could tip over and land in messy territory. She couldn't afford to let that happen. "Please, Deacon. At least let me take care of that eye."

"I'll come over but I can't stay long." He didn't say that he had to leave before Connor woke. She'd take it, though.

The minute he removed his hand from her shoulder she felt the cold air. She shrugged out of his jacket and held it out. "You need this more than I do. Follow me but take it slow to my place. I'll warm up on the run and I want to get the run in."

He didn't put up an argument, which surprised her.

She fast-walked until her legs warmed up again and then she started a light jog. It wasn't until she hit her running stride that her muscles released some tension. An argument could be made for her avoiding the trail while a murderer was on the loose. But what if her being on that trail saved lives? She wasn't exactly being discreet about carrying a gun. Her badge was clipped onto the front strap of her holster, clearly visible. She didn't want to cause a panic so she made sure everyone could see it.

Leah pushed her legs until her thighs burned. There was so much more she wanted to know about Deacon. Her heart hurt for the pain in his eyes when he'd talked about losing his girl-friend and her daughter. So much made sense now about his not wanting to be around Connor.

There was one big difference. She and Deacon weren't in a relationship. Besides, the one dat-ing rule she had was not to bring a man home to meet her son unless things were getting seri-ous. She owed it to Connor to keep stability in his life.

Rounding the corner to her block, she finally broke a sweat. It felt good. Her blood pumped through her veins and she felt alive. It was time to slow down and she slacked up on her speed. Deacon had kept pace the whole way. She half expected Dougherty's car to be parked in front of her house as he'd done when she ended the re-lationship. His temper had gotten out of control then, too. She'd been able to calm him down and get him to leave before going inside. The stress he'd been under since losing his daughter and then his wife had brought out the worst in him.

Leah held up her index finger indicating that she'd be back in a minute. Deacon held his position across the street under the lamplight where she could easily see him.

Riley was engrossed in her laptop when Leah walked inside the small craftsman-style house. Her babysitter glanced up and smiled.

"Almost done with this English essay," she said, intensely typing away. A few seconds later, she made a dramatic display of typing the last word and then closing her laptop. *"Finito."*

Leah was gathering Riley's things. She pulled out a twenty and handed it to her babysitter, who took it and smiled wider as she thanked Leah.

"How was he while I was gone? Did he wake up?" Leah asked.

"An angel. As usual. I checked on him—" she glanced at the clock on the wall "—about twenty minutes ago. He managed to find that red truck again while he was supposed to be sleeping. I literally had to peel it out of his little fingers for fear he'd conk himself in the face if he moved during the night." Riley tucked her silver laptop underneath her arm and took her coat from Leah.

Riley's forehead creased with confusion. It wasn't like Leah to rush her out the door.

"Get some sleep. You have a big day tomorrow," Leah said, urging her sitter toward the back door. She wrapped Riley's scarf around her neck until all that was visible were Riley's eyes. "And keep me posted on what happens with Drew."

"I'll take the trash out on my way. I found something, I don't even know what it was, in your fridge and it was about to turn rancid." Leah was grateful that Riley raided the fridge. She always cleaned it out and could only hope her son would grow up to be as responsible as Riley.

"Thank you." Leah barely closed the back door when she turned tail and bolted toward the front. She waved to Deacon, who was still across the street. Her heart squeezed as he walked toward her home. Not one man had been inside her house in almost four years until Deacon. This should have felt wrong but it didn't. She told herself it was because she and Deacon weren't dating and that made all the difference.

"I'll put on a pot of coffee," she said.

He followed her into the kitchen after locking the door.

"Does he have a key?" Deacon asked.

"Who? Charles?" She made a face. "No."

"I wasn't sure how serious it was before…"

His voice trailed off and she let it as she finished putting on a fresh pot. She retrieved an ice pack from the freezer and handed it to him.

"Thank you." He placed it over his left eye, wincing a little when it made contact.

The coffee maker sounded, letting her know it was ready. She poured two mugs and reclaimed her seat at the small table.

"I'm sorry about earlier, about Charles," she said before taking a sip and enjoying the burn on her throat.

"Have you considered notifying Internal Affairs Division about his temper?" There was enough concern in Deacon's voice to get her attention.

"You think he's dangerous to me?" The suggestion shocked her. Was he right? Should she notify someone at work?

"I think you should watch your back with him. You told me what he's been through and I wouldn't wish that on my worst enemy." He paused for a beat. "At the same time, going through a rough patch doesn't make it okay to stalk or threaten other people."

She hadn't really thought about it, but when he put it like that, he had a good point. "Once I go back to work, I'll talk to someone. I'll speak to the chief and see how he wants me to handle Dougherty." She'd never seen him like that before and Deacon made excellent points. She'd been so focused on the mantra *cops take care of each other* that she'd made too many excuses. Dougherty had gone too far.

"That's smart. Get something on record because he's acting out and I don't like the way he thinks he can treat you."

Leah couldn't agree more.

"How's your eye?" she asked.

"It's not bad."

Leah's cell buzzed, indicating a text. She retrieved her phone from the counter.

"Is it him?" Deacon asked with concern in his voice.

"It's from Riley's mother. She didn't come home yet. Our schedule is like clockwork and Riley always calls her mother if she's going to be late." Leah's heart dropped as she rushed toward the kitchen door.

"What the hell?" Deacon was behind her in two seconds flat. "If you stay here with Connor, I'll check the alley."

He started out the back door, pausing long enough to add, "Maybe you should call her mother and tell her to stay inside until you say it's clear."

"I'm already on the phone." Panic shot her blood pressure through the roof. Her fence gate was open and the contents of the trash bag Riley had been holding were spilled onto the lawn.

DEACON PULLED A .38 caliber from his ankle holster. He normally carried it with him on the ranch because it was the most efficient way to shoot a wild hog. Hogs could overrun a place in a flash if not kept under control. They could devour or destroy entire fields, threaten other wildlife and ruin water sources. They were also vicious. On his horse, Banjo, he always carried a shotgun but lately he'd felt the need to keep a weapon on his person at all times, considering the threat to his herd, and he had the necessary permits to pull off legal carry.

He palmed his .38 and let his finger hover over the safety mechanism as he stalked out of the opened gate. He didn't know Riley but she wouldn't be difficult to spot on this sleepy street at ten o'clock in the evening.

The air was chilly and the alley was dark. He couldn't risk calling out to Riley. If she'd been taken, she wouldn't hear and if she were hiding, she couldn't give away her spot. There were two scenarios that instantly came to mind. In one, Riley had already been abducted and was long gone. Ten to fifteen minutes could mean her abductor had stuffed her in the trunk of a car and reached the highway by now. In the second, she'd broken free and run. In this scenario she would be hiding. Her abductor could've been spooked and taken off, could be searching for her or could be hiding and waiting to strike. In any of these cases, Riley might not yell for help.

Deacon eased along the fence. He wore black

from head to toe, making it easy to slip through the alley quiet as a cat and check behind trash cans and around fences. The only noise was the occasional rustle of branches when a gust of wind whipped through the alley. He listened for any sign of Riley. Again, it was too dangerous to call out to her but that would have made this process a whole lot easier if he could.

Behind Leah's house, he almost tripped over a dark object. He crouched low and picked it up. A coat. That was another bad sign. The garbage had been dumped in the backyard and she'd dropped her coat in the driveway. There was a shiny object that he could see was her laptop.

He cleared three houses on Leah's side of the alley before reaching the end. He checked the street but it was silent. Moving quietly along the perimeter of the alley, one by one he cleared each alcove. He did the same on the other side of Leah's house. *Come on, Riley. Where are you?*

More than anything he wanted to bring that teenager back with him. More than anything he wanted her to be safe. More than anything he wanted to give Leah that peace of mind.

"I found a coat and a laptop outside." He described them both.

The corners of Leah's mouth turned down in a concerned frown. She walked over to him and took the items, cradling them like they were a child. "These belong to her."

"I'm sorry."

"Police are on the way." She set the coat and laptop on the counter. "We have to find her."

"I checked both sides of the alley and the streets. There were no cars, no lights. All I could hear was the wind." Which had picked up in the last half hour.

"Carla needs to know what's happening." She called the woman he assumed was Riley's mother as distant sirens sounded. The noise must've waked her son because a soft cry came from down the hallway.

A look of panic crossed Leah's features. Her gaze bounced from the hallway to the back door as she promised to keep Riley's mother informed.

"Will you introduce me to your son?" Deacon asked.

Confusion knitted Leah's eyebrows.

"He won't be as afraid of me if you make the introduction, and you're going to be preoccupied with finding Riley. You'll need someone to keep watch over him now that he's awake." Deacon knew the offer was risky. The kid might not want anything to do with Deacon and could make the next few minutes—hell, hours—a pain in the backside. He'd have offered to keep looking for Riley instead, but after seeing the panic in Leah's eyes, he immediately knew she needed to be the one out there.

"Right. Okay." Her eyes communicated several questions as she seemed to think better of voicing them. Instead, she said, "Thank you, Deacon."

"I'm not promising to be the best babysitter in the world but my nieces and nephews don't seem to mind me that much." He checked the area for a toy to soften the meeting as she disappeared around the corner to what he assumed was the hallway to the boy's bedroom.

Everything inside Deacon wanted to bolt out the door. He reminded himself the kid was innocent. He had nothing to do with Deacon's past. So why couldn't his stress response catch up to his mind-set?

He heard Leah's footsteps in the hallway coming closer.

The urge to bolt slammed into him as he turned toward the kitchen door, ready to make a fast exit.

Chapter Fifteen

At the last second, Deacon planted his feet and turned toward the voices coming from the hall. He figured he'd need some leverage with the kid so Deacon scanned the room again and located a stuffed dinosaur. He picked it up. Seeing Leah's kid was a gut punch.

The toddler couldn't have been more than three feet tall and looked sweet with his little arms tightly wrapped around his mother's neck. Deacon's heart fisted. This shouldn't be any different than spending time with his nieces and nephews and yet it felt on a different planet. Family was family forever. It was strange because death could take anyone away in a snap and on a rational level he knew that. His emotions were unchecked, running out of control toward a place of darkness.

"Connor, this is my friend Mr. Kent." Leah kissed her son's forehead.

The little boy looked at Deacon with red-rimmed eyes.

"Call me Deacon." He held up the stuffed dinosaur he'd found. He remembered not being able to walk through the living room without stepping on something for how many toys were scattered around on the floor at Jackie's house. He'd drop down and roll around. Emery, her two-year-old daughter, would come barreling toward him from the kitchen and then launch herself into his arms with the kind of trust possessed only by toddlers and puppies.

Connor's eyes lit up at seeing the toy. Deacon had scored a point with that one.

"Baby, some of mommy's friends are coming over to help find Riley," Leah began.

"Where'd she go, Mama?" Connor rubbed his eyes.

"She's hiding and it's our job to find her," she soothed. Leah was good with her son, Deacon would give her that.

"Do you mind if Deacon hangs around while I help look for her?" she asked Connor. He looked cautiously at Deacon.

It was now or never.

Deacon crouched down and made it look like the dinosaur was walking across the tiled floor. "Mr. Dinosaur is hungry. He's ravaging the city, looking for food and Christmas presents."

The dinosaur trampled up the leg of the table and then across it, knocking over the saltshaker that was in its path. Connor laughed. His attention was on the table, so Deacon kept going.

"Mr. Dinosaur wants coffee." He pretended to make the stuffed animal drink from the cup. Connor's laugh rumbled up and out. "What else can Mr. D eat?"

"Here. He can have a cookie." Connor rocked his body, the universal sign from a kid who wanted to be put down in order to walk. He practically threw himself toward the toy. He put his little hands on the table and Deacon's heart squeezed.

"I'll get Mr. D a cookie. One for you and your new friend, too. Okay, buddy?" She smiled down at her boy and there was so much love in her eyes.

"Yes." Connor jump-clapped, a feat mastered by pretty much every kid under the age of five that Deacon had ever met.

Leah produced three cookies, a glass of milk and a fresh cup of coffee a few minutes later as Deacon and Connor located a couple more toys to bring to the party.

She mouthed a thank-you as a knock sounded at the door. Her smile didn't reach her eyes and she was doing well keeping it together under the circumstances. Not only was she beautiful but she was intelligent and strong. She was someone he could see himself with in the bigger picture were it not for all the complications.

Besides, Deacon was in no place to start anything with anyone. He told himself all the heightened emotions they were both experiencing had intensified what he felt for her. Was he attracted to her? Yes. Would he ask her out under normal circumstances? Roger that. With the caveat of normal circumstances meaning before Jackie. Since then, single mothers were hands-off.

Deacon refocused on the kid and reminded himself not to get too attached. This babysitting gig was for one night. "Which dinosaur is your favorite?"

"Brontosaurus," Connor said with more of that enthusiasm only kids his age seemed to be able to access. He also pronounced his *R*s as *W*s, which was adorable as all get-out.

Deacon played with Connor for a solid hour before the tot started back-to-back yawns. "Hey, buddy. Do you think Mr. D is getting sleepy?"

"Uh-huh." Connor released another yawn. "But not me."

Deacon suppressed a chuckle. "Of course not. You're wide-awake."

Connor nodded. It was so obvious he was fighting sleep. For the moment he was winning but it wouldn't take long.

"How about you run and brush your teeth while I pick out a cartoon for us to watch?" Deacon barely finished his sentence before Connor issued another jump-clap. "I'll clean up in here."

Connor shrieked before darting out of the room.

It didn't take long to pick up stuffed animals and take them into the adjacent living room. It took even less time to locate a cartoon DVD. If Deacon guessed right, the kid's favorite was the one with the still-open case and the DVD inside the player. He wasn't shocked to find it was a purple dinosaur show. That dinosaur from Allen, Texas, was still going strong with the munchkin set. Memories of Emery crept in. He and her mother had dated for a year. He had been planning to introduce her to his siblings, who had no idea he'd been close to settling down.

Deacon checked his phone to see if word had come in about Riley. Even with the distraction of playing with Connor, Deacon's thoughts were heavy. It was one thing to have a murderer on the trail but now this. Could these two things be connected?

Riley had been taking out the trash. Based on her description, she looked like Leah's twin and the darkness would make it harder to tell the two apart. Leah was a capable officer but he couldn't help but worry that she might have been the target. A target, period. Her similarity to the victims of the attacks on the jogging trail where she ran might've been coincidence. Both women were similar height and build to Leah. Similar hair color. When he really thought about it, this would make Riley a target, too. He didn't like where any of this was going. More ideas churned. The women might've been killed once the attacker realized neither were Leah. And then the murderer hacked off a foot to tie the crime to the ranch. The dots were loosely connecting and he didn't like the picture emerging.

Deacon wanted to know where Charles Dougherty went after they'd left him on the trail.

His cell buzzed and he answered as Connor charged into the room.

"How's everything at home?" There was something a little too right about hearing those words from Leah.

"We're fine. Aren't we, buddy?" Deacon held the receiver toward Connor, who whooped. Deacon pushed a button on the remote, which started the cartoon and the little guy settled in next to him.

"Any luck?" He was hoping for good news.

"Nothing yet. Riley's mother checked her social media pages and called her daughter's cell at least a dozen times. She's sent texts to Riley and her friends, just in case. Drew hasn't heard from her, either. Everyone's accounted for and neighbors have joined in the search. We must've circled the block a dozen times by now." Leah sounded alert. Her adrenaline was still pumping.

"She hasn't shown here." He was stating the obvious because he would've notified Leah immediately if Riley had turned up. As much as he wanted to be out there in the search party, his job for now was to take care of the brown-haired angel that Leah had trusted him with. "Where's Dougherty?"

"He's been on the radio a couple of times. He's in on the search," she informed him.

Deacon had a bad feeling about Dougherty and it was more than just jealousy. "Keep me posted, will you?"

"I'll let you know if we see or hear anything," Leah promised before saying goodbye and ending the call.

The show's introduction song had ended and Connor hugged the brontosaurus in his little hands. The kid's smile could melt a glacier and even a hardened heart like Deacon's defrosted just a little.

The lights were dim and the environment perfect for sleeping with the TV sound on low.

Deacon hadn't slept for more than two to three hour stretches in days. He bit back a yawn as Connor curled up next to him and settled in.

Deacon didn't want to move and disrupt the kid. So he didn't.

Instead, he leaned his head back and rested his eyes.

LEAH HAD BEEN riding with beat cop Eddie Ariston for an hour and a half. Ariston was five feet nine inches and young. The deep night shift always drew the newbies. He had brown eyes, almost black hair and a solid reputation. He drove at a crawl down alley after alley in quiet Fort Worth neighborhoods adjacent to Leah's. She checked the time. Another fifteen minutes had passed. And then thirty. If they didn't find Riley soon, the odds dropped of ever locating her with each passing minute. She squirmed in her seat as she worked the spotlight, illuminating dark spots in shrubbery of the suburban neighborhood. She might do better on foot.

"Stop at the corner and let me out." She couldn't sit in the squad car and do nothing but work the spotlight for another minute. Riley could be hurt in a bush or hiding in a trash can for all Leah knew.

"You sure about that, Detective?" Officer Ariston asked, concern in his voice.

"I have a gun and my phone." She held up the latter. "Keep me posted on anything that comes over the radio."

"What if I get a call?" He was concerned that he'd have to abandon her and that wasn't something an officer would take lightly.

"Then leave me." Leah was dead serious.

"You sure, Detective?" Ariston was young but a solid cop. She'd heard good things about him and news traveled fast throughout the department. His arrests were solid.

"I'm certain," she reassured him. "You have to go, you go. I can always grab a ride from someone else. There'll be officers combing the area all night."

"If you say so, Detective." He pulled to the curb near the stop sign on Maple.

She was a couple of neighborhoods from home. Worst-case scenario she could walk the whole way or have Deacon pick her up. *Deacon.* She hoped he was still getting on fine with Connor. It should have felt odd to leave Deacon alone with her son and especially considering the fact that she never brought men home.

"Let me know if you have to take off or if there are any developments in the case," she said to Officer Ariston as she climbed out of his SUV.

"Yes, Detective."

THE CALL CAME twenty minutes later from Leah's closest work friend, Susan. Riley had been found. Leah texted Ariston, who gave her a lift to the hospital.

"Great news, huh," Ariston said as she climbed into his vehicle.

"Can't think of a better ending." Riley was alive.

"Any word on the condition of the victim?" he asked.

"She suffered facial lacerations and possibly a cracked rib." Riley was safe. Leah had to hold back the barrage of tears—tears of gratitude. After the way she left things with Dougherty, she half feared he might've confused the two of them and abducted Riley. Leah couldn't let herself go there. She couldn't let herself believe that a man who'd been in law enforcement for the better part of twenty years would be capable of such an act. Her imagination was running wild after their encounter. Riley could clear up Leah's worst fear.

"Poor kid." He paused. "Could've been much worse, though."

"She was lucky." And so was Leah. Pain from her past had roared to the surface and it was taking everything inside her to tamp down her runaway emotions.

Ariston dropped Leah off at the entrance to the hospital. She located Riley's room number and found her mother and father at her bedside.

"I'm so sorry." Leah burst into tears, surprising herself with the barrage of emotion.

Carla hopped to her feet and embraced Leah. "It's okay. She's safe."

Those words washed over Leah as tears of relief flooded through her. Carla offered reassurances that she didn't blame Leah. It could've happened to anyone.

"I'm so grateful that she…" Leah couldn't finish but the rest of her sentence seemed to be understood as Carla told Leah not to blame herself.

Leah pulled herself together long enough to move to Riley's side. "How do you feel?"

"I'm good. A little banged up. He opened the door of the trunk and pulled me out. As soon as I could stand up straight, I jammed my knee into his groin like you taught me last year. He dropped so fast and I just ran until I couldn't hear him chasing me." She smiled and then winced.

"That was super brave and I'm so proud of you," Leah said.

"I ran so far that I didn't recognize anything anymore. I was afraid to wake anyone up because I thought he could be right behind me, so when I saw headlights coming down the street, I hid in the bushes until I realized it was a cop. Then I ran toward the car, waving my arms high in the air so he could see my hands." Leah was grateful all the lessons she'd passed on to Riley had seemed to take seed.

"Your quick thinking saved your life, Riley."

The teenager tried to reposition herself but winced.

"Be careful. That cracked rib will take some time to heal," Leah said.

"Turns out it's just a bruise," Riley confided.

"Even better news." Another blessing for Leah to count in this crazy situation. "Did you get a good look at the man who did this to you?"

Riley shook her head. "He was wearing a ski mask and it all happened so fast. I kinda freaked out."

"You were amazing. I couldn't be prouder of you for defending yourself," Leah corrected. Under no circumstance did she want Riley blaming herself for the creep getting away.

"Do you think it was *him*?" Riley's voice dropped to a whisper.

"I'm not sure. The most important thing is that you're safe." Leah meant every word.

"Could he come looking for me?" she asked.

Leah feared the perp hadn't been looking for Riley in the first place. Leah was concerned that after the heated exchange with Dougherty, he flipped out. Her sense of comradery argued against the idea that a fellow officer would try to harm her. Though Dougherty had been acting irrationally lately. "I don't think so. But we'll all be more cautious after this."

"She's not leaving the house for the next few days once she's released from here," Carla stated in that voice only mothers possessed. It warned against anyone arguing. Riley seemed to catch on because she just smiled.

"I'm sure your teachers will make a plan for any missed work." Leah could almost read Riley's thoughts.

The teen's eyes sparked. "I hope so. I don't want to fall behind."

"You can always text one of your classmates to come over and help you study." Leah wiggled her eyebrows so only Riley could see. Leah could feel her guard loosening its tight grip. She was starting to breathe again. Really breathe.

Riley's eyes really lit up, as she seemed to catch on to the implication that she could spend more time with Drew.

"Where's Connor?" Riley asked, glancing behind Leah as though he might walk in the room of his own accord.

"He's with a friend." That last word tasted sour. Leah didn't—couldn't?—think of Deacon Kent as an acquaintance. And yet he'd been clear. He couldn't become serious about a woman with a child. She appreciated his honesty. Her heart had other ideas.

LEAH TIPTOED ONTO her porch. The sun would be up in half an hour and her adrenaline rush was wearing thin. She'd already seen that the lights were low inside her house. She hoped that Connor had given Deacon a break. If her son was still up, she'd let him sleep in tomorrow and go into preschool late. It wasn't like she could return to work yet and it was nice to have the flexibility for a change. Being a detective was losing some of its luster as Connor got older. At times, she felt like she was missing so much with her son. Necessity said she had to have an income, though. The long hours were becoming a grind but she told herself that would be true of any job. Part of her had been feeling unfulfilled recently. But this wasn't the time to get inside her head about it. She was tired and her mind was running with it.

She slid the key into the lock carefully. The door hinges could use some grease, so she slowly opened the door and hoped it wouldn't creak too badly.

Based on the thumbs-up text she'd gotten when she'd checked in with Deacon earlier, all was going well at home. In a perfect world, Connor would've gone back to sleep and Deacon would be stretched out snoring on her couch. She did feel guilty that his day on the ranch would've started almost two hours ago had he been home.

The light from the TV glowed through the windows. Maybe Deacon was able to grab a few hours of shut-eye. Leah suppressed a yawn. It was probably too much to hope that she would be able to get in a nap. All that mattered was that Riley was alive and could begin healing. Riley had made a startling revelation that her abductor seemed shocked when he pulled her out of the trunk, like he'd been expecting her to be someone else. The thought sat hard on Leah. But all she could care about right now was that Riley was all right.

Leah stepped inside the living room. Her heart squeezed at the scene. Deacon on her couch with Connor nestled against him. Both were out. The TV was on. The Christmas tree lights twinkled at her from behind them.

A mix of emotions nailed her and she temporarily froze. The image of her child with Deacon Kent would be burned into her thoughts from here out.

Chapter Sixteen

Deacon eased to a sitting position and rubbed his eyes. The little munchkin had fallen asleep on his shoulder and Deacon hadn't wanted to disturb him.

Opening his blurry eyes, he caught sight of Leah standing there, mouth open, mute.

He blinked at her. "When did you get home?"

"Just now." Leah jumped into action, taking a couple of steps toward Deacon.

"What happened?" he immediately asked.

"Riley's safe. Let me get this guy to bed and I'll fill you in." Leah gently peeled the child off Deacon and then disappeared down the hall.

Deacon figured this was a good time for coffee. He pushed off the couch and moved into the kitchen. The layout was familiar and he was getting to know where she kept all the supplies. It only took a couple of minutes for the machine to spit out the welcomed brown liquid. The smell alone started waking Deacon. He poured two mugs and set Leah's on the counter before checking his phone. A text from Leah an hour ago let him know that Riley had been found. She was safe.

After a couple of sips and a much-needed caffeine boost, Deacon set the mug on the counter and then stretched out sore arms. He dropped to the floor and fired off a dozen push-ups to get his blood circulating. Reclaiming his coffee, he was halfway through that first cup when Leah emerged.

"Thank you for staying with him." An odd mix of emotions played across her soft features.

Deacon handed her a steaming mug of fresh brew. "I'm just relieved your sitter was found safe."

Leah's eyes gave away her relief. "Me, too. I don't normally go there with the fear thing but I was almost out of my head with worry."

She would have blamed herself like she did with her best friend.

"What did Dougherty say about the case?" he asked.

"I haven't heard from him directly," she admitted. "But he put out word that it's even more important to find Elijah Henry…"

Deacon picked up on her hesitation almost instantly. "You don't believe that."

"No. I don't. I mean, a serial killer who starts

on the trail and then moves on to the suburbs? It's not likely." She white-knuckled her mug before blowing on the contents and then taking a sip. "Even if Elijah killed the other women, why would he be lurking in some random alley?"

"The women on the trail fit your description," Deacon pointed out.

She nodded.

"Wonder what Dougherty makes of that," Deacon said.

"I don't know what he's thinking. Honestly, he's been off for a while now." She took a slow sip of her coffee. "Chopping off a foot only complicates the matter. I mean, why do it?"

"It seems to me that someone wants everyone to believe these cases are tied to ours in Jacobstown. There've been news reports but many details have been kept out. The connection doesn't work for me."

"It'll be interesting to see what Dougherty puts in his report." Leah blew out what sounded like a frustrated breath.

Deacon walked over to her and touched her arm. "How's Riley? I don't just mean physically."

"She'll be okay." Leah shrugged off his concern.

He caught her stare. "You don't have to blow things off with me. How is she *really*?"

"Scared. It was traumatic." She blinked and slicked her tongue across her bottom lip, leaving a silky trail. "It might not be the same thing or to the same scale but I know what she'll go through, especially if she believes she's the only one who survived this guy."

"Even more reason to find the truth." Deacon's list of people he wanted to talk to was growing. Dougherty was off-limits. Talking to him would only get Leah in more trouble with the chief. He didn't need to add to her troubles. "Where does Elijah stand in all this to you?"

"Still a suspect. Although, he's moved to the bottom of the list. I'm guessing Dougherty will move him up the list again after this." She issued a sigh. "You know how people get locked on to an idea and then they can't see anything else?"

"Happens all the time," he said.

"Even to us, right?" She glanced up at him.

"Yeah. Sure. Why?"

"I think Dougherty's lost his objectivity. I mean, he's locked on to Elijah being guilty and he won't see past it. He could be like that before with cases, I'd noticed. Don't get me wrong, he used to be a great detective," she quickly added.

"And now?"

She shrugged. "You saw him earlier. We've all been covering for him. He makes mistakes. We all try to catch them. There's no way any of us would allow an innocent person to go to jail. Probably the person closest to Charles is Keeve." She glanced up with an apologetic look when she must've realized he had no clue who that was. "Detective McKeever. You met him at the diner. We all call him Keeve for short."

Deacon had a few words for that guy the next time he saw him because he was certain Keeve was the one who'd notified Dougherty that Deacon and Leah had walked in. "I remember."

"I should circle back and ask him what Dougherty thinks is going on." She took another sip of coffee and Deacon had to fight the urge to kiss the drop of brown liquid on her bottom lip.

"You didn't see Dougherty tonight, right?" he asked.

"No. Not personally. Not since the trail."

"He wasn't on the radio?" he pressed.

"I heard him at one point. Everything happened so fast I guess I wasn't thinking about it. Why?" Her forehead creased. "What are you trying to say?"

Deacon paced a couple of rounds in the kitchen. Logic said an officer of the law would never consider doing what Deacon was about to accuse Dougherty of. Deacon stopped and stared at her. "He's fixated on you."

She stood there for a long moment and he could almost see the wheels turning in the back of her mind. She opened her mouth to speak and then shut it down almost as quickly.

"Hear me out before you make up your mind one way or the other. Believe me, I don't make this allegation lightly." Deacon fully understood the sense of family that law enforcement officers shared. His cousin, Zach McWilliams, was the Broward County Sheriff after all. "He has it in for you. He's been trying to get you in trouble ever since the breakup. His attitude toward you, toward women in general was off—"

"He would never try to hurt me if that's what you're saying," she interjected.

"I don't know what I'm saying just yet. He's covering for something. He's not thrilled with you. How far would he take that? I don't know. Maybe there's someone else involved, someone who has it out for you and Dougherty's looking the other way." Deacon was thinking out loud. He knew how absurd this would sound to an officer. Police work was all about being family. He also knew how rare it was for one of their own to turn because of the bonds created in the life-or-death situations faced by each of them on a daily basis. If an officer went bad, it was the worst kind of betrayal.

And the most dangerous, a little voice in the back of his head reminded. The person would be smart, and trained with a weapon and police tactics. Luckily, it happened so rarely that it almost wasn't worth considering. Except everything had to be examined in this case and Elijah Henry didn't strike Deacon as the murdering kind.

Leah seemed to let Deacon's words percolate. And then she marched over to the table where she'd set her phone down and fired off a text.

LEAH STARED AT her phone, waiting for a response.

"Who are you reaching out to?" Deacon asked.

"Keeve. He's been watching over Dougherty. He might know where Dougherty was tonight or what he's thinking," Leah said. Either way, she needed to come up with a new plan because there was no way she'd put Riley at risk again by asking her to sit with Connor and she was her only sitter. She picked up a napkin and shredded it, waiting for a response. Keeve was most likely asleep.

Her cell tones shocked her. She immediately picked up when she saw the caller's name, Keeve.

"What's going on?" she said into the phone.

"What the hell do you think you're doing asking that question?" Keeve started in.

"I'm trying to find out where Dougherty was tonight. I'm creating a timeline of events so that I can—"

"This is not your case." His tone was final. Was he kidding?

"When my babysitter is a target, everything about this is my business. First, my jogging trail and now my sitter. Come on, Keeve. No matter how much you're on his side you can't deny the coincidence," she argued. From the corner of her eye, she could see Deacon tensing up as the conversation intensified.

"He was with me. Are you accusing me of being involved now?" Keeve's anger was out of place.

"I'm trying to get to the truth. What's up with you?" There were many other choice words she wanted to say to him but thought better of. Nothing said in anger ever turned out well. She'd learned that lesson with her parents. Shouting at them had never helped them understand what she'd been going through. In fact, it only made everything worse. The more anger poured into a situation the further the two sides divided, until building a bridge seemed impossible. That was pretty much her relationship with her parents in a nutshell.

Keeve issued a sharp sigh. "This case. It's awful. I don't like any of it. Dougherty was with me earlier. I dropped him off at his house not long after you texted me before to ask where he was."

"Thanks for telling me, Keeve." She couldn't exactly rule Dougherty out or discount the possibility he could be responsible.

"He hasn't been right lately. I'm not making excuses for the way he's been treating you, Leah. You're a damn fine detective. Let a little steam blow over before you parade another man in front of him, will ya?" Keeve crossed the line.

"I wasn't *parading* anyone in front of him. The last time I checked, you called him to let him know where I was the other m—"

"I wouldn't do that to you or him," Keeve interrupted. He sounded sincere, which confused her. If Keeve hadn't let Dougherty know about her at the diner, then who had?

Since going down that path wasn't productive, she decided to steer the conversation back to the investigation.

"Keeve, does he still think Elijah Henry is responsible?" Why not go ahead and ask? She figured it couldn't do any further damage.

"I believe so," he said.

"Riley's almost eighteen years old, Keeve," she said. "And this is all a little too close to home."

"Some of us have volunteered to run extra shifts. One of us will be patrolling your street at all times," he stated.

"Why didn't I hear about this?" she asked.

"We take care of our own, Leah. You know that." It was true enough.

"Thank the guys for me if I miss anyone." For the first time in years, she wasn't sure it *was* safe to be home. She had Connor to consider and his safety meant everything to her.

"I will." Keeve's promise helped her feel better about her ties at work.

Leah ended the call and looked at Deacon. "You know why about eighty percent of murders involving women are solved?"

He shook his head.

"Because a woman is almost always killed by someone she's intimate with—a husband or a boyfriend. Most of the time we arrest the man who kills a woman." Leah fought the tears welling up. "There's no connection between these women aside from size, height and similar looks."

"Except that they are similar to you. Riley, who is also similar to you, got away." Deacon crossed the kitchen again. "I can't help but think attention's going to the wrong place."

Leah's phone dinged with a text.

"A pair of witnesses just identified a picture of Elijah Henry as being seen near the trail on the night of the second murder." Leah couldn't believe it.

"Any chance you can get the names of the witnesses who've seen him so far?" Deacon asked.

Leah could get into serious trouble for checking into Dougherty's case again. On balance, she had to know for herself. Besides, she needed to see if Dougherty was hiding something. She didn't really believe—or maybe she just didn't want to believe— that he could be capable of doing what had happened earlier. "Something's bothering me."

"About Elijah?"

"Dougherty. I mean, he knows the cases. If someone's trying to wrap these murders up with the animal slayings, they're cutting off the wrong foot. Dougherty wouldn't make a mistake like that. He's too good of a detective and I can't believe that he would try to hurt me." Maybe she was being naive. But her fellow detectives were like her family, and whether she and Dougherty were getting along or not, she couldn't imagine that he would ever threaten her life.

"I don't know." Deacon stood there, looking at her, examining her. His gaze was…*appreciating her*?

Leah was still trying to shake the image of Deacon with her son from earlier. The picture kept replaying in her mind. Granted, she hadn't brought home any men to meet her son that she'd dated. Did he somehow wish he had a father?

She needed to tell him and remind herself that Connor very much had a father. One whose memory she would make a point to keep alive for her son. There were pictures of Wyatt in Connor's room. Leah wondered if she should put some in the living room. Until now, she hadn't really thought of what her son might be missing out on.

Although, now wasn't the time, either. Because it was looking more and more like if a killer had his way, Connor would be without both parents. Nothing in her could allow that to happen to her boy. Connor deserved to have a family, dammit.

Tears sprang to her eyes. They were unexpected and embarrassing, considering Deacon was still there. She hadn't really cried since losing her husband. Leah couldn't afford to let her emotions run wild. She couldn't risk letting them get out of control. If it were just her, she could let them go berserk. It wasn't. Connor needed a stable and strong mother. One who made it clear that he was loved unconditionally.

Deacon walked toward her and then thumbed away a hot tear streaking down her cheek. "What is it? What's wrong?"

"I'm sorry. I don't usually…" She blinked up at him.

"Cry?" Deacon cocked a half smile. "It's one

of the most natural things. Why should you apologize for that?"

With Deacon standing there in front of her, so close she could reach out and touch him, she felt safer than she had in her entire life. Was it dangerous to allow that feeling to envelop her? Maybe. Right now, in this moment, all that mattered was looking into his honest steel-gray eyes and seeking comfort in his arms.

"Should I apologize for doing this?" She pushed up to her tiptoes, wrapped her arms around his neck and kissed him. At first, her lips barely pressed against his. Even so, she could smell the dark roast coffee on his breath. He brought his hands to rest on either side of her hips and his touch was tentative.

"Or how about this?" She nibbled his bottom lip as he raked in a breath.

"This is not the best idea right now." His voice came out raspy and a trill of awareness shot through her at the fact that he seemed to want this, too.

"Is it wrong to do this?" She pressed her body flush with his and heard another rasp before she pressed her mouth more fully to his. This time, she slicked her tongue across his lips, enjoying the taste of coffee.

He groaned when she pulled back enough for cold air to take the place of warmth between them. He stared into her eyes like he was trying to read her mind.

"I want this, Deacon. Do you want me, too?"

"You've been through an ordeal tonight. You're tired and I don't want you to wake up tomorrow and have regrets." His voice was low, gravelly.

Was he worried about her having regrets or him?

"I know my own mind, Deacon. And I think you know yours. We aren't the kinds of people who jump into something irrationally. What do you want?"

She stood there, daring him to tell her the truth.

"You want to know what I really want?" he asked.

"Yes." Boldly, she held on to his gaze.

"I want to kiss you again. Hell, if I'm honest, I want to do a lot more than that but there's a little munchkin in the next room who could wake up at any second. And once I start down that road with you, I don't want to take a chance we could be interrupted."

Chapter Seventeen

Leah disappeared into the next room and then returned a few seconds later with an electronic device in her hands. "He won't wake up, but even if he did, we'd hear him long before he got out of bed by using this."

Deacon recognized the monitor from a similar one at his oldest brother's house. The sound was crystal clear and, thankfully, one-way.

He took in a sharp breath, needing to be fully aware of what he was about to do. "If we don't stop now, it'll change things between us."

"I know this is going to sound strange but I feel like I've known you my entire life. And certainly not like a brother. I've never felt these kinds of feelings with any other man before. I've never allowed myself to. But, now? I want to know what it'll be like and I sure as hell hope things change between us after *this*." She pushed up onto her tiptoes and brushed a kiss against his lips. "And *this*."

Deacon looped his arms around her waist and dipped his head down to claim her mouth. He pressed her against him, hard. With her body flush against his, he could feel her wild heartbeat—a beat that matched his own. He covered her mouth with his and teased his tongue inside her mouth. She parted her lips for him and reached back to grip the counter. His hungry tongue drove inside her mouth and she pushed up to sit on the counter, wrapping her legs around his midsection.

She released her hands from around his neck and smoothed her flat palms along the ridges in his chest.

His hands, rough from work outdoors, trailed along the V in her shirt, pausing at the top button. He hesitated for a second, another threshold that once crossed couldn't be undone.

She must've sensed his hesitation because she immediately unbuttoned that top button for him. He groaned against her lips once and then again as he ran his finger along her silky bra.

Deacon pulled back enough to capture her gaze. She was so damn sexy with her dark hair and eyes.

And then he took care of the rest of her buttons, fast; with nimble fingers he navigated down her shirt. She shrugged out of it and it landed on the floor. She brought her hands underneath his shirt and smoothed them across his skin.

Within a hot minute, they stood naked in the kitchen.

"You're beautiful," he said in barely a whisper as she smoothed his flat hand across her belly. Her skin goose-bumped underneath his touch, causing rockets of awareness to shoot through him. "So beautiful."

She blinked up at him and said, "So are you."

And then she let her hands roam free on his chest, his shoulders. He kissed her again, harder this time, tasting all the sweetness. His body shook with need and he could feel hers tremble under his touch.

He traced her collarbone before cupping her full breasts. Her back arched and he swallowed her moan. He tugged at her nipples, rolling one between his thumb and forefinger as sexual tension built toward an urgent pitch inside him.

"You're sexy, Leah," he said into her ear.

"You make me feel that way," she responded, looking him straight in the eyes. "I want to feel you inside me, Deacon."

That was all the urging it took for him to wrap his hands around her sweet round bottom and pick her up. She gripped the counter behind her and the motion caused her breasts to brush against his chest. She wrapped her legs around him as he took one of her breasts in his mouth.

He rolled his tongue around the tip of her nipple and she arched her back. He could feel that she was ready for him, so he positioned her sex on his shaft. She wiggled her hips until he reached deep inside her and then matched him stride for stride.

Their bodies matched up like they'd been made to be together. Deacon's mouth found hers and he drove himself deeper inside her.

His body was an electric battlefield as she bucked her hips and dug her fingers into his shoulders. And damn, Deacon had had plenty of sex in his life but this...*this* was beyond comparison. Everything in his life righted itself and he had the overwhelming feeling of being right where he was supposed to be. *Forever?*

When they both couldn't seem to get enough air and he felt her internal muscles convulse, Deacon let himself dive off the cliff, too.

It took a while for their breathing to slow. They just stayed as still as they could, holding onto each other as though neither wanted to let go.

DEACON PUT ON a fresh pot of coffee while Leah finished her shower. He knew he was in trouble with her. The sex they'd just had felt like anything but the raw animal magnetism he was used to. Don't get him wrong, it was all that and more. The emotional connection they'd shared had brought their lovemaking to a whole new level and that caught him off guard. Had something stirred inside him immediately when he'd met the detective? Yes. But this was too soon for real feelings. The only relationship he could compare it to was that of his and Jackie's. He'd loved Jackie. Hell, he'd been ready to make a trip to the ring store before...

Deacon cursed.

He couldn't think about Jackie right now. Shoving his feelings down deep, he poured two fresh mugs of coffee.

Leah walked in and stopped as soon as her gaze landed on him. "What's wrong?"

"Coffee?" He held up a mug.

She didn't take it right away. Instead, she studied him and he felt for a second like she could see right through him.

And then she walked to him, kissed him and took the mug.

"You haven't really slept," he said to her, dodging her question.

"I'm fine. My adrenaline is off the charts and I learned to get by on power naps after Connor was born." Leah looked beautiful in the oversized pink cowl-neck sweater she'd put on over a fresh pair of jeans. She was brains and compassion and internal beauty wrapped up in one package.

"I'd like to circle back and speak to Dougherty's witnesses on the Jillian Mitchell and Delaney Richards cases," Deacon said. She seemed ready to cut him some slack when she nodded.

"It shouldn't be too difficult for me to get hold of those names," she said. "I was thinking we should review their statements but on second thought we should follow up ourselves and see what they have to say."

"Dougherty could be sloppy—"

"Distracted," she interjected.

"Either way, I don't trust his investigative skills right now." Deacon searched her eyes for understanding. At the very least the man wasn't being thorough. Women were dying, and from what it looked like, Leah was a target. Which brought him to his second point. "I'd like you to stay on the ranch while this case is active."

"Impossible. I go back to work in three days and Jacobstown is too far away in the countryside." Her jaw muscle ticked and he could see that he'd hit a nerve. Then, it hit him why she'd have that reaction. Of course, she'd want to stay close to Riley.

"I can't ensure yours and Connor's safety here. We have help there so you can focus on the case, and someone will be around 24-7 to help with your son. Meals will be taken care of, so there'll be no distractions." He hoped he could sell it to her based on the practicality of the suggestion. Down deep, he wanted her close to him.

"He'll feel strange away from his home and especially if I'm not there." Her walls were constructed high again. He understood the reason. She wasn't quite ready to let anyone else in her and Connor's lives. It had been the two of them for three years and she'd been handling everything on her own. There was comfort in that. Plus, Deacon had rerouted the conversation when she'd asked him what was wrong.

"There's enough distraction on the ranch to keep him occupied. There are other kids close to his age to play with and more animals than you can count. I haven't met a kiddo yet who wasn't ready to pack a bag and move in once he or she was on the property." He took a couple of steps toward her and tucked a stray strand of hair behind her ear when he got close enough to. "I need to know that both of you are safe. I can't do that here. Not even if I stick around, which I'd planned to if you'd let me. And, I'm not trying to force you to do something you're not comfortable with. Although, if I'm honest, I like the thought of you and Connor in my home."

She opened her mouth to argue but clamped it shut.

"We have supplies on the ranch so you won't have to think about anything for the day-to-day. You can devote all of your time to Connor and the case."

The contents of her coffee cup became really interesting to her. She was a reasonable woman and it was a solid offer. So why wasn't she jumping all over it?

The reason dawned on Deacon a few seconds later. "The killer's not forcing you out of your home. He's not winning. This is about making smart choices and keeping that little guy in there safe." He looked her square in the eyes because she needed to know how serious he was about this next part. "I care about you and I need to know that you're safe. I won't be able to go back to that life, to leave you, if I think there's a chance *he* could get to you or Connor."

LEAH THOUGHT ABOUT what he was saying. Granted, he was one hundred percent right about not taking unnecessary risks. She would do whatever it took to protect Connor. "I want to stay here to keep an eye on Riley. I feel like if I leave, she could end up in more danger."

The comment seemed to strike a chord with

Deacon. "Any chance you could ask a fellow officer to stay at Riley's house for a few days?"

"No one will be available given the hunt for the killer."

Deacon nodded. "I can send someone to stay at her house if you think her parents will agree."

"It never hurts to ask. Her mother trusts me." Leah fired off a text to Riley's mother, Carla. The response came quickly. "Carla said she wouldn't mind a little extra security until this guy is behind bars. She said she thinks Riley will sleep easier, too."

"Does that mean you'll come home with me?" Deacon asked. He dipped down and kissed her. "Because I want you to."

A dozen butterflies released inside Leah's chest. And if she set aside the emotional piece, he'd made solid points. She wouldn't be throwing in the towel, surrendering to a bully and cowering. It was smart to know when to stand her ground and when to take help being offered to her.

In this case, Deacon was right. As long as Riley had extra protection, Leah would take him up on his proposition. "I'll come to the ranch. I think it'll be a nice change for Connor and we both could use some fresh air."

Deacon's smile lit his face and he looked even more handsome if that were even possible. She liked being the one to put that smile there. He went straight to work on his phone, no doubt scheduling the security person to keep watch over Riley. His fingers flew on the cell's keypad. He lifted his eyes to meet hers and asked, "Do you think we should wake Connor now or wait until he wakes naturally?"

"I'll gather toys and pack a suitcase for both of us. If he's not up by then, we'll wake him. I don't want him to get too off schedule today or he'll never sleep tonight." Working as a real team felt good to Leah. Even with Wyatt she'd never felt this kind of... She didn't know the right word for it... *Ease?* Ease seemed too simple to define the dynamic. Ease didn't come anywhere near approaching the physical draw to Deacon or the way her stomach fluttered every time he was in the room.

The sex had been all fireworks and something more. She'd never experienced sex that had blown her mind in the way it had with Deacon. There was so much more than physical attraction. Although, there was plenty of that, too.

But enough thinking about that. This case would end. Feeling as defeated as she did right now, being no closer to the man responsible for murdering women made it important to remind herself of that fact a hundred times a day if that's what it would take. She would return to a normal life. A heavy sigh slipped out as she busied herself locating a few of Connor's favorite toys.

She packed up his DVDs after digging around for their cases. He repeated them so often it did no good to put them back properly after each viewing.

She zipped Connor's bag, wondering how things would be when the case was solved. Would she be returning to a life before Deacon? It seemed so empty and hollow now.

A FEW IDEAS about the case rolled around in Deacon's head. None he liked. His mind was locked on to Detective Charles Dougherty. Had he snapped? Granted, it was unlikely but that didn't mean it was impossible. The officers on the force today mainly came from military backgrounds and were the first to have seen real action. No one knew what impact that would have on their psyche. Therefore, it was unknown just how many were affected by their service overseas. Sure, they had to pass mental testing but that didn't mean much. How many times had his cousin Zach spoken about his concern for his deputies' well-being, physical and mental? The effects of stress during military service were only beginning to surface in police work.

Deacon didn't have to ask Leah to know that Charles Dougherty had served. He could tell by the way the man carried himself. Deacon couldn't name which branch based on being in the same room with a person for five minutes, but he knew when he came across someone who'd been overseas. Dougherty's service made it that much more difficult to put the man in any other light than a good one. Deacon had nothing but respect for his fellow servicewomen and men.

But his internal alarm bells had sounded off after meeting the guy. Dougherty was possessive of Leah. He was angry. He'd suffered the worst kind of trauma with his child. He'd lost his wife. And then possibly the last tether he had to reality, Leah, when she'd ended their relationship. That could send a man who was already on the edge tumbling off, which wasn't an excuse by any means and it didn't make any of his behavior acceptable. Deacon could follow the logic. That's all. He'd seen good women and men come back broken after serving overseas. The effects didn't always show right away.

The most difficult part was that a soldier had a hard time asking for help. In part because he or she was trained to handle anything. And anything and everything happened across the ocean. Deacon counted himself fortunate that he hadn't brought demons back with him. Because he'd seen people stronger than him crack. It didn't make him better than the others. It only made him luckier. Everyone had a breaking point. He'd come home before hitting his.

"Everything okay?" Leah stood at the doorway to the kitchen studying him.

"Dandy." He hoped she'd let him get away with that and not dig deeper. She had a way of getting to his core and he'd never been so readable to anyone else before. He found that he did want to tell her something more about himself. Not his suspicions about Dougherty but about Deacon, the man. "I served in the military after high school."

"Thank you for your service," she said without hesitation.

"You're welcome." There was no hesitancy on her part when she walked over to him and kissed him, either.

Deacon couldn't help but feel a deeper connection with Leah. She understood so much without him detailing out his background. She'd lost someone she cared about, too. He knew that about her. But even if he hadn't, he'd have seen it in the pride in her eyes right now.

"Guess I wanted to make my own mark on the world. I did a stint and then bounced around from job to job before I met Jackie. Her little girl, Emery, had the brightest smile. She was two years old when a car struck them at an intersection and killed both on impact." Deacon had never been able to talk about Jackie and Emery before, not with his family or friends. It was easier than he had expected it to be with Leah. She felt like the calm in a storm. Was it because they were two kindred souls? Two people who knew what real loss was?

"I'm so sorry, Deacon."

Was that the tether binding them so tightly? Or was there so much more to their bond? He'd tried to dismiss the notion he could fall for someone so fast, or that he could open his heart to anyone.

Could he let Leah in?

Chapter Eighteen

The Kent family ranch was so much more beautiful and grand than Leah had expected. Warmth radiated from the main house, which was one of those two-story brick Colonials with white columns on a front porch that went on for days. The place looked like something out of a Southern-living style magazine and the lands surrounding it were even more stunning. The air smelled cleaner in Jacobstown, Leah noticed as she breathed in a lungful.

Connor beamed as he took in the scenery. As soon as she let him out of his car seat, he bolted toward the house and toward a black cat that was lounging on the porch.

"Gretchen won't mind the company," Deacon said, motioning toward the animal who was stretched out on her side. Connor dropped to his knees beside her and scratched her belly. "Looks like she found a new friend."

"He loves pretty much all animals," Leah said,

just out of earshot of Connor. "He'd love a dog but we're not home enough. It hardly seems fair."

"We have a few to choose from on the ranch if you change your mind. People come out to the country and leave behind all manner of animals," he said with disgust.

"That's awful." Leah couldn't believe it but then she'd seen even crueler sides to people.

"A dog could go on your nightly run with you. Bring some peace of mind," he offered.

"I've thought about that, actually. But I'm never home. I feel badly enough that Connor attends his preschool's aftercare program. I barely get to see him, let alone an animal." If her schedule ever slowed down or she changed careers someday, getting a dog would be high on her list.

"Let's go inside, buddy," she said to Connor.

He frowned until Deacon told him there were more animals inside the house.

"What's her name?" Connor asked. To him, every animal was female because of Pickles.

"Gretchen," Deacon supplied.

The smile on Connor's face would have melted a glacier. And that's exactly what the temperature felt like. It might have been cold outside but there was a fire crackling in the main house's fireplace and the smell of cookies baking in the oven. Heaven? Leah couldn't think of a more beautiful family home to grow up in.

The place was grand, even by Leah's standards. The house she'd grown up in might've been large and well-appointed but it lacked the warmth of the Kent home. Leah was a little nervous that Connor wouldn't take to the place and a lot nervous that he would. She would never be able to give him this or anything in this hemisphere. A voice in the back of her mind reminded her that all a kid really needed was love. It was true. Love and maybe a dog. She smiled at the thought. Someday.

Leah picked up her son and he hugged her around the neck. "Sweet boy."

Deacon introduced her to his four brothers, one sister and two cousins. One by one each family member welcomed her. Then came the little ones. They were the twins, Aaron and Rea. The second he saw them he tried to wiggle out of Leah's arms so he could get down and play. The next thing she knew he was racing past on a tricycle, showing off to the twins.

"Connor, slow down," she warned.

Deacon waited until her son got out of earshot before he leaned in and said, "It's okay with us if you want to let him go at it full force. Our folks brought us up allowing play inside. They said they didn't want to live in a museum and loved the sound of children's laughter. Since we grew up that way, we never think twice about letting a kid be a kid. Of course, we always brought our best manners to the supper table. That was nonnegotiable."

"We're like that at home. I guess you already know that because of the state of my house." She figured it was as good a time as any to explain the chaos of toys all over as if he hadn't already noticed.

"I reckon the two of you will fit in just fine here." He chuckled. It was a low rumble in his chest. This wasn't the time to notice how that chuckle was a light feather roaming her exposed skin, leaving a trail of goose bumps.

Leah needed to cool it right there. Being in Deacon's home with his family around for protection was one thing. She didn't need to mistake his hospitality for anything more serious. Especially with how much her heart protested. She liked his family. They were down to earth and not pretentious like her own parents. She'd always been an only child so she had no idea what it was like to have siblings. After seeing the Kents, she was starting to realize just what she'd missed out on.

Would Connor miss out on a father figure and siblings, too?

"I better call Susan and see if there are any updates on the case." Leah excused herself to call her colleague. The two had hit it off immediately when Leah had made detective. The occasional lunch was as far as their relationship went, though, because Susan was married with four kids under the age of eight. She had no free time outside of work.

Leah found a quiet spot on the back porch. The days were getting shorter by a minute or two every few days this time of year and she missed the extra sunlight. She pushed a stray strand of hair out of her eyes and focused on the screen. She scrolled through the names in her contact list, allowing her finger to hover over Wyatt's name. She probably should've deleted it a long time ago. Someone else had to have been assigned that number by now. A strange slap of reality struck. It would be incredibly strange to call this number and hear someone else's voice.

She had so many wonderful memories of Wyatt. He might not have been the man of her dreams but he'd cared about her and made her want to care about someone else again in the process. Their relationship might not have been perfect or even for the right reasons but she got an amazing kid out of the deal. And that wasn't half bad. In Connor, she would always see Wyatt. He would always be with her. It was time to let go. Leah plucked up the courage to delete the number before calling her friend.

Susan picked up on the second ring. "Hey,

girl. I've been worried about you. I'd ask where you've been but I heard the story of what happened last night near your house from five people already."

"It's been a roller coaster," Leah admitted.

"How're you holding up?" Susan lowered her voice and Leah realized her friend was most likely trying to sneak away from ears that might be listening. Susan was used to seeking privacy. She'd joked dozens of times that she couldn't even go to the bathroom by herself after having the fourth child.

"What's the word on Elijah Henry?" Leah figured she might as well get straight to the point of the call.

"No one can find him to ask where he's been the past few days. In fact, he's completely fallen off the radar ever since his release," Susan said.

Leah's gut braided. "You really think it's him?"

"Me? I'm still following the evidence trail. It's too early to determine his guilt or innocence. I don't like his connection to you, though." Susan paused a beat. "You don't remember him, do you?"

"Elijah? No. Why would I?" Leah asked.

"I was talking to Keeve yesterday or the day before and he said you arrested Henry like five years ago," Susan supplied.

"Wait. Hold on a minute. *I* have a history with Elijah Henry?" she asked.

"Yeah. According to Keeve you do." The news had the effect of a bullet through the chest.

"What else did he say?" Leah couldn't wait to hear this. Why didn't she remember Elijah? Maybe if she'd been the one to talk to him instead of sending in Deacon to see him face-to-face, she'd have remembered. After the pregnancy she'd pretty much lost half her memory due to the onslaught of hormones.

"Guess the guy had it out for you after the arrest. It caused him to lose his job and then his ex got full custody of their kid. He had supervised visitation after... You don't remember any of this?" Susan sounded surprised.

"Not a bit. That's a familiar sob story, though," Leah countered. "And I can't count the number of people who've threatened me after arresting them. Pretty much every drunk and lowlife I came into contact with."

"True. This guy seemed to have it out for you in particular." She paused another beat. "How many times do we ask ourselves about this? If one of our old arrests came back for us, which one would it be?"

"You'd think it would be someone I remember, at least."

Susan blew out a breath. "Seriously."

"I need a favor," Leah hedged.

"What is it?" Susan's voice quieted again.

"The names of the witnesses who saw Henry in the area." She knew she was asking a lot. And she would never put her friend in a bad position if it weren't life or death. "But if you're not comfortable—"

"I'll give the names to you right now," Susan said.

"Are you saying you already have the names?" Leah was stunned and very grateful.

"I've been expecting your call. I have names, addresses and phone numbers. I would be asking the same thing if the situation were reversed. I mean, I'm not saying Dougherty is a bad detective but he's gone a little bonkers with everything he's been through. He's not in his right mind and I don't think he's doing his job," Susan said. Almost the exact same words Deacon had used to express his doubts.

"You won't get an argument from me." Leah felt the same. Dougherty was being sloppy and her life might depend on getting this right. At the very least her professional career hung in the balance.

"Dougherty has been saying that Elijah is close to confessing but he couldn't hold him and they had to release him," Susan said.

"Elijah?"

"According to Dougherty, the man all but claimed responsibility." Susan sounded worried.

"Do you believe him?" Leah could trust Susan with an honest answer.

"I want to." She issued a grunt. "Mostly, I want this to stop. This is creepy. You know? And not just because I feel like it could've been you and now with your sitter. The whole thing gives me a bad feeling."

"Me, too." Leah didn't like any of this whether she was ultimately the target or not. None of it felt good and people were dying. "The families of those murdered women deserve answers. They deserve to know what really happened and who did this."

"I know." Susan's tone was quiet now, like they were in church.

Leah got the names before ending the call. She typed them into the notepad feature of her smartphone. She heard the door open to the screened-in porch and knew Deacon was behind her. A moment of panic seized her as she turned to face him. "Is Connor all right?"

"Connor's great. He's laughing and rolling around on the floor with Aaron. Rea moved on to her dolls. The little guy fits right in here and even though there's an age difference I think Aaron likes having another boy around," Deacon said. She picked up on something in his voice that didn't match his words.

Did he regret bringing them home to the ranch?

"I have news," she said.

"I ARRESTED ELIJAH HENRY five years ago and he says his life went downhill after." Leah was wringing her hands.

Deacon took her hands in his. "Your friend Susan told you this?"

She nodded, looking straight into his eyes. For the first time, he saw confusion.

"What else did she say?" he asked.

"That everyone thinks Dougherty's too distracted by his personal issues to do a good job on the case. And that he swears Elijah was about to write a formal confession." The guy Deacon visited hadn't seemed anywhere close to admitting murder.

"Elijah flat out told me he was innocent. I can't believe he'd change his tune," Deacon pointed out.

"Did you mention my name to him?" she asked.

"Not specifically." Deacon thought about it for a minute. "I'm not an investigator but I do have a decent gauge of whether or not someone's lying to me. I got the impression that Elijah was scared and that he believed he was being set up."

"He's a drunk," she said.

"He'd be the first to admit it," he added. "He seemed truly scared, like something big was going down and he was knee-deep in it."

She studied him. "You're sure that wasn't just him being afraid because he'd done horrible things? I've seen a lot during my years as a cop and now detective. People make all kinds of crazy statements and then recant later. People aren't always as they seem."

"It's best to let the evidence lead us," he said. "I'm interested in seeing what those witnesses have to say."

"So am I." She produced a text from Susan with names, addresses and phone numbers. "We have a twenty-year-old *musician* as a witness." She made air quotes when she said *musician*.

"None of his bandmates saw anything?" Deacon asked.

"He's a street musician. Plays drums for dollars and change. I've seen him before. He plays at a different spot every night. He's also been picked up multiple times for disorderly conduct and being under the influence of drugs," she supplied.

"It's four o'clock," Deacon said. "Probably too early to catch him out."

"We can head downtown. He likes to play next to a taco shop."

Deacon checked the map feature on his phone. "Who else? Anyone on that list seem respectable?"

"There's a bouncer, a vagrant by the name of George Washington, and a married father of two. Nick Chester works in some kind of marketing job and lives in Frisco," she supplied.

"The dad sounds like the most credible source," Deacon said. "Him and the bouncer."

"Jax Hanks is twenty-four years old. He's the doorman at The Sloppy Pig, which is a place we watch constantly for drug traffic." She caught Deacon's gaze. "The suburban father is our best bet. We'll still interview the others. You never know what will break a case open."

He'd heard that before from Zach.

"Are you sure about us staying here?" Leah asked. "Stepping in to help a stranger is one thing, but this is above and beyond. Taking us in and volunteering to help with Connor. I can't remember the last time I saw him this happy. He's a happy kid, don't get me wrong, but this is…"

"My family can be overwhelming but they're good people. Last I checked on them, Connor was happily sharing his brontosaurus with Aaron, who was in absolute awe," he said, and he couldn't help but smile. He liked that she and Connor fit in so well with his family.

"Kids are so in the moment," she said on a sigh. "I always wonder if that's the key to their happiness. I mean, if they're upset, they throw a temper tantrum. Granted, I could do with less of those all-out throw-himself-on-the-floor tantrums that he used to have and seems to have thankfully outgrown but there's something smart about not stuffing emotions deep down."

She looked at Deacon who could relate.

"When they're happy, they just let it all loose. You can see it radiating from them," he agreed.

"There was one time Connor's body literally vibrated with happiness. It was a couple of weeks ago and we were waiting in line to see Santa. Connor was so exuberant it was like he couldn't contain it," she continued.

Could he live life in the moment? Not worry about tomorrow? Just enjoy being?

Her smile made him wish he could because it was sexy as hell and he wanted to spend more time in the moment with her.

"Your family has been amazing, by the way," she said as he brought his hand up to her chin. He tilted her face toward his and looked into her eyes.

"Good. Because from the looks of it, they're enjoying having you both here," he said. He was happy.

For how long?

Chapter Nineteen

The drive downtown didn't take long. Deacon was getting awfully familiar with the highway leading to Fort Worth from Jacobstown. Part of him wanted to argue that he felt more at home in the city than he did on the ranch. That couldn't be true, though. Could it?

Deacon loved the land. He loved his family even more. It was probably his stubborn streak rearing its ugly head that had him wanting a life outside of it all. Granted, he would always love his family and he wanted to be connected. He just needed to figure out where he fit in the big picture of the ranch. He didn't have the passion for it like his oldest brother, Mitch, and his baby sister, Amber, had. His brother Will had fallen somewhere in the cracks of ranch life, too. Nate and Jordan were the other two of Deacon's brothers who were questionable. They had lives of their own, and Deacon figured he should talk to them and see where their heads were in regards to moving to the ranch full-time.

It was already getting dark by the time Deacon and Leah arrived downtown. Dinner had been served at the ranch and Connor had been bathed before Deacon and Leah had headed out.

Connor took to the ranch and Deacon's family, and part of him wondered if it was such a good idea to mix his worlds in that way. Even though he'd been with Jackie for a year, she'd never met his family nor had Emery. He figured they could all meet once he popped the question and she said yes to being his wife. Looking back, it seemed odd to him now that he hadn't wanted to bring her home to his family. Had he thought she wouldn't fit in?

Did a part of him realize that he loved her for the wrong reasons? That he'd fallen in love with the three of them as a family? He and Jackie rarely had time alone until Emery had gone to sleep. He would've done anything for that little angel. *Including marry her mother*, that annoying voice in the back of his head stated. Damn. Was that true? Had he confused loving the three of them as a family with loving Jackie? Because she'd never stirred his heart or mixed up his emotions as much as Leah.

The first stop in the downtown tour was an underpass beneath I-30 along Lancaster Avenue to find George Washington, dubbed GW. Deacon bit down the irony that he was searching for a homeless man who shared the same name as the first president. Deacon also figured the man had mental health issues, as so many homeless people did. He wanted to know more about GW and possibly help the man if he could.

There were a couple dozen blankets laid out with grocery shopping carts dotting the landscape. The place smelled like urine and days-old garbage.

"What's going on down here? Why are there so many people?" Deacon quietly asked Leah.

"Budget cuts hit the city hard. Quite a few shelters shut down a couple of months ago because grants were tightened up. Money has been hard to get," she said. "It has especially affected our citizens dealing with mental health challenges. People who don't have families to take care of them."

Deacon wasn't naive and he didn't live in a vacuum. Well, he sort of did. The ranch was a safe haven and Jacobstown was the kind of place people moved to in order to get away from crime in the city. He'd grown up in a sanctuary compared to most. He got that. Serving his country was the first time he'd seen the other side of the coin. He was proud of his service, and it had opened his eyes to life outside the bubble. His parents had been generous souls and had devoted themselves to various causes. His mother had had a huge heart and soft spot for sick children, animals and people with disabilities. All of the kids had been brought up to help their fellow citizens. Deacon's mind was already reeling as to how he could help.

"These people need food and shelter." Deacon also knew that many had developed drug or alcohol dependency. His personal belief was that anyone who wanted help should be able to find it. "A rehab program would do a world of good here."

"I can connect you with people who can help you set that up if you're serious," Leah said quickly. "That's the worst part of my job. I see all this need and I can't do much about it. Let's face it, arresting people after the fact doesn't help with the reason they did whatever crime they committed. I'd love to see more prevention measures that would make my job obsolete. I got started in law enforcement to make a difference to victims' families. And now, after all I've seen, I think my time would be better spent making sure no one ever had to go through this in the first place. Does that sound strange?"

"Makes perfect sense to me," Deacon said reassuringly.

A couple of occupants were scattered around.

Leah walked up to the first one they came to. It was an elderly-looking woman who was hunched over her shopping cart. She glared at Leah and Deacon while spreading her arms over the contents, like she expected them to rob her.

Seeing this was heartbreaking. Deacon knew right then and there he had to do something.

"You know anyone by the name of George Washington? Some people call him GW," Leah said to the woman. Leah pulled out her badge and showed it. The woman relaxed her grip on the cart.

"Haven't seen GW since the other day," she confessed.

"Any idea where I might be able to find him? He's not in trouble. I just have a few questions about something he witnessed," Leah said.

The woman shrugged bony, rounded shoulders. "Haven't a clue."

"Do you know him?" Leah asked.

"As well as anybody could, I reckon," the lady said.

"What can you tell me about him?" Leah's voice held compassion and respect.

Deacon appreciated her manner with people. He could see that she was a good detective. *And a good mother*, that voice in the back of his head reminded. He told the voice to be quiet.

"He sleeps over there." She pointed to a spot next to a pylon.

There wasn't much there from what Deacon could tell. Did the man sleep on the ground with no coverings? On second glance, Deacon saw a hint of color. Whatever it was couldn't have been big enough to cover a grown man.

"Where's his blanket?" Leah asked.

"Doesn't have one. He sleeps sitting up. It's the strangest thing but he swears it helps—" she flashed eyes at them before continuing "—keep his mind clear. Says if he lies down, the ants'll crawl into his brain."

It was clear that GW had issues.

"Do you have any idea when he'll be back?" Leah seemed to already know the answer to the question but had to ask anyway.

"There's no check-in time here at Casa Royal." The older woman swept her arm across the air as though presenting a room in a five-star hotel to distinguished guests. She grinned, obviously pleased with herself for making a joke. "Haven't seen him in at least two days."

"If you do see him, will you give him one of my cards? He's not in trouble. I just need a few minutes of his time." Leah pulled out a card from her handbag and handed it to the woman. "Thank you."

"Anytime. And bring handsome back if you

come again." The woman snickered, clearly feeling like she was on a roll.

Leah walked over to the spot GW called home. An army jacket was folded over next to the column. Leah picked it up and dusted it off. The name patch read *Washington*.

Knowing a veteran slept in these conditions was a gut punch to Deacon. He pulled out his phone and began making calls in order to set up a temporary shelter and provide food. That would accomplish phase one of his plan—a plan that was taking shape as he followed Leah away from the makeshift home for what had to be three dozen folks or more. If any one of these people wanted help, they'd have it.

Leah was quiet the rest of the way to the car. Once inside, she started the engine and then sat there, staring out the front windshield. "You have a habit of going around rescuing people? That some kind of Cowboy Code or something?"

"I can't fix every problem. No one can. But I have a moral obligation to help anyone I meet who is in need of a hand up. It's not a Cowboy Code. It's being a decent human being." Deacon meant it. His parents hadn't brought him up to turn a blind eye to someone in need and he was fortunate to have the resources to follow through.

"That why you're helping me? Moral code?"

There was defeat in her voice and it took a minute for the reason to dawn on him.

"At first? Yeah. Something like that. But, now? I'm here because I have feelings for you, Leah. Feelings that are too new for me to be comfortable talking about them. All I know is that I need to know you're going to be safe. I need to know Connor will be okay. That's as far as I can let myself go right now."

"Oh." He hated the sound of disappointment in that one word.

"Can we just live in the moment? I'm doing my level best not to get too inside my head. I like the feeling of being around you. There's something different when I'm with you. Is that enough for now?" He sure as hell hoped it would be because he couldn't imagine walking away, and somewhere down deep he knew it was a lot more than just her well-being that was a magnet he didn't want to pull away from.

LIVE IN THE MOMENT. Leah had been thinking the same thing earlier. Why did it feel somehow less than that to her now? She wasn't ready to get inside her head, either.

The club would open soon.

"Jax should be at The Sloppy Pig by now." She took in a deep breath. "Ready?"

"Let's roll."

The Sloppy Pig was a ten-minute drive from the underpass. The ride over was quiet. The air was still when Leah exited her vehicle.

She walked toward the bar. A feeling of the world righting itself came over her when she felt Deacon's hand on the small of her back. It was probably a mistake to allow the gesture, the physical contact, to comfort her. It did.

The Sloppy Pig was one of those nightclubs with a DJ and several dark corners to congregate in. There were plenty of country and western bars in the area. This place wasn't one of them. There was an edgier crowd here. People wearing mostly black clothes with dyed-black hair and multiple piercings patronized this place. Leah and her fellow officers knew The Sloppy Pig because it was a good place to scrounge up informants. Motorcycle gangs frequented the place.

The burly-looking young man in his late twenties who stood in front of the entrance was most likely Jax. Leah pulled her badge from inside her pocket and held it out as she approached. "Jax Hanks?"

The guy's face paled. "Am I in some kind of trouble, Officer?"

That was a strange reaction from an innocent man. She held on to the thought but pushed it aside for the moment.

"Not if you haven't done anything wrong," she stated.

Jax's gaze shifted from her to Deacon and she could tell Jax was sizing Deacon up. Yeah, Deacon was taller and more muscular. Jax looked like a linebacker from a college frat party, tall with a round middle and strong. In a fight, Deacon would take Jax and the bouncer seemed to know it.

Jax crossed his arms over his chest. "What's going on?"

"You witnessed a man leaving a crime scene the other night. I believe you spoke to my colleague, Detective Dougherty…" Leah hesitated at Jax's reaction to the detective's name. His left eye twitched. Leah didn't like the implication that Jax was afraid of Dougherty.

"Yes, ma'am." The guy's voice was tight. Unraveling him and getting anything out of him had just become more difficult.

"Can you tell me what you saw?" she asked.

"I already gave my statement. There any reason I need to give it twice?" His hesitation didn't sit well. Was he trying to remember what he said?

"Where were you exactly when you saw the man you identified leaving the crime scene?" If she fired a few questions at him, maybe she could loosen him up.

"It's in my statement." He looked at her with blank eyes. "Do I need a lawyer?"

"No. Why? Should I take you downtown to answer my questions?" She stood there boldly in order to let him know she wasn't intimidated. There was no way she would do what she said but he didn't know that.

"I'm good here." He wasn't giving her much to work with. His responses gave her the impression he was afraid to talk. The way he'd buttoned up the minute she'd mentioned the case didn't sit well.

"Then why don't you start answering my questions?" She had no real leverage so she softened her approach.

"I took a walk because the weather was nice." He flashed angry eyes at her. "I got a lot going on, trying to save for school, and I've been having roommate trouble. I live with a couple who broke up and it's messy. I needed fresh air after being inside our place with them."

"Where did you go?" At least he was talking. She could check his answers against his statement later.

"On the trail," he supplied like she should know that already.

"Any specific spot? It's a big trail," she continued.

"Near the bend. I didn't hear anything but I saw a man acting weird," was all he said.

"How? What was he doing?" She didn't like

the fact that his answers seemed rehearsed. He wasn't giving away more than he had to. Was he afraid he'd slip up?

"He wouldn't look at me. He kept to the shadows. That's why I noticed him in the first place. He seemed... I don't know... Creepy. He had long greasy hair like he hadn't washed it in a few days and he looked surprisingly strong for a man who was so skinny." Jax's answers bothered Leah for a couple of reasons. His voice was even. He was giving too much detail—people always gave too much detail when they were lying.

"I thought you said he kept to the shadows?" she reminded Jax.

Leah didn't have a copy of his report but experience told her his statement would be almost exactly what he was saying to her now. Because on instinct she could tell he was lying.

"I've said everything I can remember. Maybe you should talk to this guy." Jax pulled a business card out of his wallet. It belonged to Dougherty. Leah bit back a curse.

"Thank you for your time, Mr. Hanks." Leah turned to Deacon. "We've heard enough."

Deacon nodded and she appreciated that he seemed to know when to speak and when not to. She turned before she cleared the area and looked back at Jax one more time.

"Hey, Jax," she said.

"Yes, ma'am," came the response.

"I'll be back to check on this place. You know, make sure everything's running legit and no customer gives you a hard time." It was a veiled threat that he would understand. She was saying that he needed to keep his nose clean or she'd find a reason to haul him in.

"Look forward to seeing you again." His voice hitched and she could tell that she'd struck a chord. Good. She didn't need him talking to Dougherty as soon as she disappeared.

Deacon didn't say a word until they were inside her vehicle. Then came, "He didn't see anything."

"You picked up on that?" She was impressed.

"His reaction to your presence. The way he remembered too many details but said he was in the dark. My question is why? What does he have to gain?" Deacon asked.

"Good question." Leah put the key in the ignition. "Maybe we'll get more from Nick Chester."

The drive to Frisco took longer in traffic. Nick Chester lived in a two-story house on a suburban street of newly built homes. The row of houses was similar with brick-and-stone facades. Every house on the block had two stories and a solid-wood door. The yards were similar in size and scale, and trees were nothing more than saplings. The word *cookie-cutter* came to mind as Leah looked at the endless stream of similar-looking homes. She figured not much would be different on the inside of the places. This was the land of carpools, Suburbans and 2.5 kids.

A twinge of jealousy struck Leah that was so out of the blue it caught her off guard. Because behind those wooden doors were real families. Holidays with tables full of parents and grandparents, and pretty much everything Connor would never have.

Leah looked at Deacon as they got out of her vehicle.

He stopped and froze. "Everything okay?"

She shook off the reaction she was having as a bout of *Saturday Evening Post* nostalgia. Those families could be dysfunctional. She'd been called out to play referee on countless holidays when crazy Uncle Billy decided to pick a political fight with conservative Aunt Jean.

"Yeah. Fine." She palmed her badge and walked toward the front door. This neighborhood had a front-entry garage, a relatively uncommon concept in this area that was meant to maximize backyard space.

Leah knocked on the door. She heard a male voice shout that he had it and she assumed he meant the door.

An attractive man in his midthirties answered. A TV blared a familiar cartoon in the background. The man was tall with a runner's build and sandy blond hair combed over in the front that made him look like he could be from a well-known democratic Massachusetts family.

Leah flashed her badge. "Nick Chester?"

"Yeah. This is his place. Hold on a minute. I'll get him," the surprised-looking man said. He partially closed the door until only a crack of light peeped through. Leah had no grounds to go inside when she wasn't expressly invited but she knew something was up. And then a minute later the garage door was opening.

She and Deacon turned around from the front entry in time to see a luxury sport utility come roaring out. Leah ran toward the vehicle but it was too late. She couldn't catch Nick in time to stop him.

Chapter Twenty

"I knew that man was Nick." Deacon cursed under his breath as he turned to face Leah.

"Me, too. We have no right to be here but those are the actions of a man guilty of something." Frustration seemed to pour off her in waves. "I don't like the picture emerging. We have a vagrant witness who suddenly can't be found. Another witness, a bodyguard at a nightclub, emerges who seems scared to speak to a detective after seeming to have no problem pointing the finger at Elijah Henry. And now the other witness bolts before I can interview him. Dougherty's case against Elijah Henry feels like a setup."

"We can always see what Nick Chester's wife thinks is going on." Deacon's suggestion was met with a nod.

Leah knocked. Her badge was still in her left palm, a habit she'd picked up early on in order to keep her right hand free for her weapon.

An attractive woman answered the door with a surprised expression. She was roughly five feet four inches. Her shiny wheat-colored hair was pulled away from her face in a ponytail.

"Mrs. Chester?" Leah asked.

"Yes, Officer. What's wrong?" Mrs. Chester looked like she expected bad news, like Leah was there to tell the woman someone close to her had died. She didn't look guilty or suspicious. If Mrs. Chester had been the witness, Leah would've gone home and waited for a conviction for Elijah Henry. That wasn't the case here.

"Your husband answered the door a minute ago and then took off. Did he say where he was going?" Leah figured she'd get right to the point.

"He said we were out of milk. Why do you need to talk to him?" The concerned woman's brows knitted.

"May we come in?" Leah could only ask.

"Um, sure." Mrs. Chester opened the door wider and led them into the open-concept kitchen.

Two kids, both under the age of eight, were sprawled out on the floor. The youngest stared intently at the cartoon and the other at an electronic device.

"I'm sorry to interrupt your evening, Mrs. Chester—"

"Please, call me Abby."

"I'm Leah." She offered her hand. "This is a friend of mine."

Deacon introduced himself.

After courtesies were exchanged, Leah decided to get down to business. "Where was your husband last Tuesday?"

Abby picked up her phone on the counter and checked the calendar. "Let's see. I had a meeting at Carol's school that night, so he would've been here. No. Wait. That's not right. I had to ask the neighbor to sit for me because my husband had a work thing downtown."

"What kind of work does your husband do?" Leah asked.

"He heads up marketing at Bellamy Insurance," she supplied.

"Is it common for him to take meetings at night?" Leah pressed.

"Yeah. Sure. He's downtown almost once a week for something. He meets with advertisers and they like to take him out to dinner." She stared at them. "Is my husband in some sort of trouble?"

"Did he tell you about witnessing a man leaving the scene of a murder?"

Abby gasped and brought her hand up to cover her mouth. Her gaze darted to the girls on the floor in the adjacent room.

"I'm guessing the answer to that question is no," Leah continued when Abby didn't speak.

"I had no idea." Abby's gaze darted around before landing hard on the cell in her hand.

"Do you have any idea why your husband would keep that information from you?" The only reason Leah could think of was that he was hiding something.

"No."

"Can you get him on the phone and ask when he'll—"

The cell in Abby's hand buzzed, cutting off Leah's question. It was Nick.

Another gasp issued from Abby. "Can I—"

"Yes. Would you mind letting him know we have no plans to leave until he comes home?" Leah hoped the statement would work.

Abby did as she was instructed. The call ended within a minute of starting. "He'll be right here. He said that he panicked and he's sorry."

Leah thanked Abby.

Nick walked through the door leading to the garage a minute later. He must've been at the end of the street, waiting.

Sweat beaded on his forehead. His bronzed skin had paled. He raked his hand through his hair. "I apologize for earlier."

"Mr. Chester—"

"Call me Nick. Please."

"Nick, where were you last Tuesday evening?" Leah dove right into her first question.

Nick's gaze darted from his wife and back to Leah. "Can we talk out back?"

"I have a right to know where my husband was," Abby protested.

The anguished look on Nick's features intensified. "Honey, I'm sorry."

"What have you done, Nicolaus?" Abby's voice shook in fear.

He took a minute to speak and Leah figured he was drumming up the courage. "It started off innocent enough." His gaze trained on his wife. "I swear I never meant to hurt you. I love this family."

"Who is she? Do I know her?" All the color had drained from Abby's face.

Nick shook his head. "It's not like that. It's not emotional."

The younger kid called for mommy. For a split second, Abby looked torn. "We'll talk later." She moved into the next room, shoulders slumped forward.

Nick watched, a mix of embarrassment and grief playing out in his eyes. He lowered his voice. "I never should've gotten involved with Anastasia."

"Is she a working girl?" Leah put it delicately.

"It's not like that. She dances at Fire and Ice

Gentlemen's Club," he said almost under his breath. "One of my clients started taking me there six months ago."

"Is that where you were last Tuesday evening? The club?" Leah asked.

He shook his head.

"You were with Anastasia, though." Leah's statement was met with a nod.

Abby picked up their youngest and carried the little girl upstairs. "Where were you?" Leah asked.

"Her place."

"Does she live nearby?" Leah already knew the answer to the question.

"Yes." The man's face looked purely tortured.

"Is that where you witnessed the man you identified leaving the scene of a murder?" Leah pressed. "Did he have blood on his clothing when he emerged from the woods? Did you see Elijah standing over the body?"

Nick just stood there, mute. He looked like he was engaged in a serious mental debate. "Is he in jail?"

"He will be. Possibly for a very long time with your testimony." There was a crack in Nick's face that Leah needed to explore. "Why do you care? The man cut off a woman's foot after murdering her. Doesn't he deserve to be locked away?"

Nick issued a sharp breath. "Whoever did that should be given to his victim's families for them to decide the punishment."

"Are you saying the man you identified isn't the killer?"

DEACON LISTENED AS Leah took apart the so-called witness. The picture playing out wasn't a good one. It meant that Charles Dougherty had coerced a witness. Why?

"The detective threatened to tell my family what I'd been up to if I didn't go along with what he said," Nick stated. "I had no idea I was identifying a murderer."

Nick's wife stood at the bottom of the stairs, listening. She called for her eldest daughter to turn off the electronic device she'd been playing with and get ready for bed.

The little girl put up a protest but obeyed her mother in the end. Nick stood by, looking helpless and alone.

Deacon had no idea what Nick and Abby's relationship was like. The only evident fact was that both of their lives were about to change. Nick's secret was out. It would be up to the two of them what they wanted to do with it. Along with Nick's anguish came a sense of what looked like relief. Secrets ate away at the person who held them.

"If you tell the detective that I've recanted, he won't leave this alone. I threatened to tell my wife. Honestly, I was sick of leading a double life anyway. It's been eating me up inside. I'm not making excuses for my actions. They're wrong. But I wanted help and didn't know how to ask for it. I didn't know how to shatter my wife's world when she found out that she'd married a jerk who had let her down." Nick's responses came off as genuine. He'd messed up big-time. Only Abby could decide if their relationship could overcome his mistakes.

The situation hit Deacon hard. How many times had he wished he could go back and change the past? How many times had he wished he would have asked Jackie to marry him? Losing her and Emery had knocked the wind out of Deacon.

Granted, he wouldn't have cheated on Jackie. But would he have made her happy? He could be honest enough to realize that he'd fallen for the family, which was Jackie and Emery. He hadn't necessarily fallen in love with Jackie herself. Deacon tabled the thought for now.

"I appreciate your honesty," Leah said to Nick.

"Am I going to be arrested now?" he asked.

"Not if you recant your statement." Leah looked at Nick with compassion. "I'll make sure you don't receive backlash from the detective who cornered you into your statement. It's a criminal offense to provide false information in an investigation."

Nick nodded.

From the stairwell, Abby said, "He'll do the right thing. Won't you, Nick?" It wasn't really a question. She had a suitcase in her hands that she set at the bottom of the stairs. "I'm putting the girls to bed and I want you to be gone when I'm done."

"Honey—"

"Don't call me that." Her voice was laced with controlled anger. "We'll talk tomorrow. Tonight, I need to process what I've heard. In the meantime, you can show me that you're serious about figuring us out by making sure an innocent man doesn't go to jail for the rest of his life."

Nick immediately turned to Leah. "I'll change my statement and do whatever it takes."

Was this enough evidence to prove Elijah Henry's innocence? Speaking of which, the fact that he hadn't turned up yet was gnawing at Deacon's insides.

"I'll be in touch with instructions of what to do next," Leah said after exchanging information.

First things first, Deacon figured she'd want Nick to speak privately with the chief.

Deacon's cell buzzed. The call was from his older brother, Mitch.

"What's up?" Deacon asked, figuring Connor must be awake.

"Security caught a man on camera illegally hopping the fence on the east lawn of the ranch," Mitch said. "Everything's under control but I thought you and Leah would want to know."

"Thanks for the information," Deacon said to his brother. "Keep me posted if anything changes."

"You know I will," Mitch said.

Deacon said goodbye and ended the call. He looked at Leah. "A man tried to trespass on ranch property."

"Was he caught?" Panic brought her voice up an octave.

"I'm afraid not. It could be nothing, but—"

"We need to get home," she said.

Before he could respond, she was making a beeline toward the front door.

Chapter Twenty-One

Leah updated the chief on the situation with Dougherty while Deacon drove. Deacon feared that there might be blowback from Chief Dillinger for her inserting herself into Dougherty's investigation but the chief seemed to listen, and based on her responses the man seemed to trust her.

The rest of the drive was quiet.

Leah pinched the bridge of her nose and leaned her head back as though staving off a headache.

Deacon would never forgive himself if someone got through security at the ranch and somehow got to Connor. Hell, if anyone on the ranch ended up hurt or worse because of Deacon's plan, he'd never forgive himself.

"I'm sorry to put your family at risk because of me," Leah said. "I should've thought this through better. At this point, Dougherty is either slipping as a detective or is a murderer. If it's the latter, then he has nothing to lose."

"It's not your fault," Deacon countered.

"Then it's not yours, either," she stated.

That was probably fair. Deacon still blamed himself. He pushed the gas pedal harder.

"I just wish we were there already." Leah tapped her foot on the mat.

"We'd know if anything else happened. We have a solid security team on the ranch," Deacon told her.

"It's just hard to be away. I keep worrying about Riley or other women on the path. What good does it do for Dougherty to convict an innocent man?" And then it seemed to dawn on her what Deacon was thinking. "He's been after me this whole time?"

"That's my best guess," Deacon stated.

"Why? What's his motive?" She genuinely seemed stunned.

"You told me once that murders involving women are almost always solved—"

"Because the person who kills them is intimate with them," she finished his sentence. "Why didn't I connect those dots before?"

"You trusted him. He was one of your own and it's unthinkable what he's doing," Deacon said.

"The women on that trail… That was supposed to be me," she said.

"Best I can figure is that he had to act fast in order to surprise the victims. When he realized he had the wrong person the first time, he chopped off her foot to throw everyone off. I'm guessing he thought if it happened on the trail, the murder would seem random."

Leah's body visibly shuddered at the idea that Dougherty had planned to kill her all along.

"He was getting desperate after his mistakes. The heat was on, so he went for a direct attack," Deacon continued.

"But he got Riley instead. She fought him and got away and that's when his witnesses started disappearing." Leah relayed the timeline of events. "The chief said he'd call Keeve and see if he knew where Dougherty might be."

Neither said the man at the ranch could be him but it was obvious that they'd thought it—thought it and feared it. A man with a gun, police training and a badge wasn't someone to be taken lightly.

Deacon turned onto the two-lane highway leading to the ranch. There were no streetlights in this part of the country so he put his high beams on. An object rocketed toward them from the woods, crashing into his windshield.

The vehicle fishtailed as Deacon nailed his foot to the brake. There was enough momentum for the vehicle to spin out before landing in the ditch and wedging onto its side. Leah un-hooked her seat belt at the same time as Deacon. Both jumped into action as the crack of a bullet split the air.

"Get out of the car before he blows it up," Leah shouted.

"Roger that." Deacon had the window down and helped her out the driver's side in a matter of seconds. His military training kicked in and had him covering her as they moved toward the opposite side of the road. He stayed low and scanned the area for any signs of a flash or the next shot being fired.

"You have your cell on you?" he whispered to Leah. His was inside the vehicle.

"No. All I have is my gun," she responded.

"Same." He pulled his .38 caliber from his ankle holster. Backup would have been nice but between the two of them they had ex-military and current law enforcement against one man.

"You betrayed me," came an angry voice from across the road. It belonged to Dougherty.

"We're friends, Charles," Leah responded.

"Can you keep him talking?" Deacon spoke barely above a whisper.

"I'll try," she promised.

"If you get a clear shot, take it," he whispered.

"You do the same," she said.

He kissed her before moving quietly through

the underbrush away from her. Deacon didn't want to split up but their chances improved if he tracked the voice. Was it possible that Dougherty didn't know that Deacon was with her? He'd been driving her vehicle.

"We can still be friends, Charles," she shouted, breaking the silence.

"You're a liar, Leah." Deacon tracked the voice about thirty feet east from Dougherty's last location.

"I'm sorry if I hurt you, Charles. I never meant that," she continued, and he could tell that she'd stayed put.

Keep at it, sweetheart. Keep him talking.

The wind whipped around and the temperature had dropped a good ten degrees since leaving Frisco. Forward progress was slow for Deacon. Patience won this kind of battle. Deacon had firsthand knowledge of the fact. But facing down an enemy while protecting the woman he loved was new. *Loved?*

Yeah. Deacon was in love with Leah. And when they got out of this mess—because he couldn't allow himself to think it might end any other way—he'd tell her how he felt. For now, Deacon listened. The only thing that could be heard was the rustling of evergreen leaves.

"Charles? Let's talk about this." The fear in

her voice shot through Deacon. He wanted—no, needed—to protect her.

"You're a bad person, Leah. The department must be cleansed," Dougherty finally said after several tense minutes. He'd changed positions and was about twenty feet away from Deacon based on the nearness of Dougherty's voice.

Deacon froze. One wrong move and it was all over for him. The thought of Leah facing Dougherty alone pumped a shot of adrenaline through Deacon. He steadied his breathing and didn't move an inch.

"I've made mistakes, Charles. Does that make me a bad person?" Leah asked.

The quiet was deafening. Deacon thought he saw movement to his right but it was just a branch dancing in the wind.

"I HAVE A son to think about, Charles." Leah was fishing for Dougherty's location. "Connor needs me. A young child needs his mother."

It was a risky move, bringing up children. But she couldn't stand the quiet and was trying to get a reaction from Charles so that Deacon could find him. Was he close?

More silence, save for the winds that were picking up. And then a commotion was made in the brush about twenty feet away from her. Leah reacted, bolting in the opposite direction.

Leaves slapped her face as she pushed through the trees. She had no idea where Deacon was and she was making too much noise tromping through the underbrush.

She slowed her pace instead.

"Do you really think you're punishing me by killing innocent women, Charles?" She was trying to get a response from Charles and also letting Deacon know her new location. She crouched low and moved as quietly as she could.

"They weren't supposed to die. They got in the way." His voice had no feeling. He was like a robot.

"You chopped off the wrong foot, you know," she stated.

"That was my mistake," he countered.

"And what about Elijah Henry? Did he get in the way, too?" She was goading him. If she kept him focused on her, then Deacon could get to him.

"They'll never find his body."

Leah gasped.

"Society is better off without one more leech on the system." Charles had snapped. That was for sure. He'd been under duress but none of this sounded like the man she'd known, the man she'd tried to be a friend to. Could she remind him about his daughter? Somehow bring him back from the dark place he'd gone?

"Kiera wouldn't want her father to hurt anyone, Charles. Have you thought of her?"

Silence.

She'd struck a chord. Was it the right one? Leah didn't realize she was holding her breath or white-knuckling her Glock until the blow to her back came and air gushed out.

She fought for control of her Glock as the barrel of Charles's weapon pressed into her forehead.

Out of seemingly nowhere, Deacon rammed into Charles and knocked him off balance. Leah scooted back until her backside slammed into a tree and felt around on the ground for the gun that had been knocked out of her grip.

Her eyes were still adjusting to the pitch-blackness of the countryside but she heard the struggle between the two men.

She popped onto all fours and felt around in the underbrush in order to locate her Glock. If anything happened to Deacon...

Leah couldn't go there. A crack sound was followed by a flash of light. "Deacon!"

All she could hear was the sound of punches landing on body parts and grunts. The car wasn't too far away. If she got to it, she could get help on the way. Nothing in her wanted to leave Deacon alone with Charles. Without her weapon, she felt defenseless.

Leah moved closer in order to get a better look and assess what was going on. Both men wore black and she couldn't tell one from the other. The fight was real, though. It was still on. She raced toward her vehicle and located Deacon's cell. They were close to the ranch and his family would be able to get there quicker.

She remembered that Mitch lived on the property and so she located him in the contacts and made the call.

Mitch answered on the first ring.

"This is Leah. We were ambushed after turning onto a two-lane road. Charles is here, he's armed and we need help." The words rushed out all at once. "Shots were fired but I don't know if Deacon was hit."

She could barely process those words.

"I know where you're talking about. I'm on my way." Sounds of rustling came through the line. "Wherever you are, stay put. Backup is coming."

"I'll call 9-1-1." Mitch would be closer than a cruiser, which is why she'd made that call first. Her hands were shaking from another shot of adrenaline but she managed to make the call to dispatch and relayed the same information.

Within a few seconds she heard sirens in the distance.

Movement came from the tree line. Leah's

heart pounded her rib cage as she knelt beside her vehicle. "Deacon?"

It took another few seconds before she heard his voice—the voice that belonged to the man she'd fallen in love with.

"You're safe, Leah," he said.

She jumped up and ran toward him as he dragged an unconscious Charles out of the trees.

"You're okay." She threw her arms around his neck as he let go of the man he'd been pulling.

"I love you, Leah."

And then Deacon collapsed.

"No. No. No." She dropped to her knees and began checking him for signs of blood. It was too dark to see clearly so she felt around his body for anything that might be wet. His thigh was soaked and she prayed help would arrive as she rolled him onto his back, cleared his airway and prepared to administer CPR.

"Deacon. Talk to me." She felt for a pulse. "No, Deacon. Please, come back to me."

A vehicle roared up next to hers. Mitch and Will came rushing toward her.

"I can't tell if he's breathing," she shouted.

Mitch was opposite her in a heartbeat. "Come on, brother. Wake up."

The rest was a blur of lights and sirens. Zach showed up, as did an ambulance. Deacon's brother Will reassured her that Deacon was breathing as they watched from the sidelines as EMTs went to work. At some point someone put a blanket around her shoulders. Charles was cuffed and placed in the back of the sheriff's SUV.

And then Deacon was placed on a stretcher that was rolled into the back of the ambulance.

Chapter Twenty-Two

"The doctor said you should be in bed," Leah said to Deacon. He'd convinced her to wheel him out to the back porch at the ranch. A couple of the windows were open and the air was warmer than the last time she was in this room a week ago.

Deacon had taken a bullet in the thigh and it had nicked an artery. He'd lost a lot of blood but, thanks to his physical condition, was already recovering. Dougherty had been charged with the murders after confessing to everything. Elijah was found alive and was recovering.

The sounds of nature came alive at night on the ranch, she'd noticed. It was a different life than in the city but she refused to leave Deacon's side until he was better.

Plus, Connor loved being on the ranch.

"I have a confession to make," Deacon said as he repositioned in the chair.

Leah's heart raced. "What's that?"

"I'll be up and around soon," he hedged. What was that look on his face? Was he about to tell her that it was time for her to leave? He'd said that he loved her before he collapsed. Did he mean it? Or had he been delirious?

After spending a week taking care of him, being with him in his home, she couldn't take hearing the words from him. So, she preempted. "Connor and I should probably get back to our lives in the city soon."

Deacon didn't respond.

"Is that what you want?" he finally asked. "Because the confession I have to make is that I've fallen in love with you."

She started to speak but he put a hand up to stop her.

"Some people might say that this is rather sudden." He looked her in the eyes. "They'd be wrong. I knew there was something special about you the first time I saw you. I wasn't ready to open my heart again to anyone. But logic didn't matter. The heart knows what it wants. Mine wants you, Leah. What do you say? Do you feel the same or am I wasting my breath?"

Leah kissed him.

"I've been waiting my whole life to love you, Deacon. I didn't know that before we met. But I've never felt this way about another person before and I want to spend the rest of my life figuring out what that means with you," she said.

Deacon pressed his lips to hers. He pulled back enough to say, "Did you just ask me to marry you?"

"I don't know. Would you say yes if I did?" She couldn't suppress her smile or the happiness bursting through her insides.

"I'd get down on one knee but that's tricky right now." Deacon pulled her to his chest and kissed her. "I wasn't sure I could ever be happy living here on the ranch, but with you and Connor I've finally found where I belong."

"I want to live here if it's okay with you. Connor loves it here and I love being surrounded by family," she said.

"What about your job?"

"I got into law enforcement to make a difference in people's lives. You made a few calls to set up programs for the homeless. Any chance I could get involved in those projects?" She pressed her lips to his.

"You can do anything you like as long as you come home to me every night." He chuckled that low rumble from deep in his chest. Leah placed her head over his heart and listened to the sound of it beating.

This was home. He was home. Everything else could be figured out as they went.

"I'm ready to get that dog now," Leah said.

* * * * *

Look for more books in USA TODAY *bestselling author Barb Han's Rushing Creek Crime Spree miniseries in 2020!*

And don't miss the previous books in the series:

Cornered at Christmas
Ransom at Christmas

Available now from Harlequin Intrigue!

Psst!

We're Getting a Makeover...

STAY TUNED FOR OUR FABULOUS NEW LOOK!

And the very best in romance
from the authors you love!

The wait is almost over!

COMING FEBRUARY 2020

Get 4 FREE REWARDS!

We'll send you 2 FREE Books plus 2 FREE Mystery Gifts.

Harlequin® Romantic Suspense books feature heart-racing sensuality and the promise of a sweeping romance set against the backdrop of suspense.

FREE Value Over $20

YES! Please send me 2 FREE Harlequin® Romantic Suspense novels and my 2 FREE gifts (gifts are worth about $10 retail). After receiving them, if I don't wish to receive any more books, I can return the shipping statement marked "cancel." If I don't cancel, I will receive 4 brand-new novels every month and be billed just $4.99 per book in the U.S. or $5.74 per book in Canada. That's a savings of at least 12% off the cover price! It's quite a bargain! Shipping and handling is just 50¢ per book in the U.S. and $1.25 per book in Canada.* I understand that accepting the 2 free books and gifts places me under no obligation to buy anything. I can always return a shipment and cancel at any time. The free books and gifts are mine to keep no matter what I decide.

240/340 HDN GNMZ

Name (please print)

Address   Apt. #

City   State/Province   Zip/Postal Code

Mail to the **Reader Service:**
IN U.S.A.: P.O. Box 1341, Buffalo, NY 14240-8531
IN CANADA: P.O. Box 603, Fort Erie, Ontario L2A 5X3

Want to try 2 free books from another series? Call 1-800-873-8635 or visit www.ReaderService.com.

Get 4 FREE REWARDS!

We'll send you 2 FREE Books plus 2 FREE Mystery Gifts.

Harlequin Presents® books feature a sensational and sophisticated world of international romance where sinfully tempting heroes ignite passion.

FREE Value Over $20

YES! Please send me 2 FREE Harlequin Presents® novels and my 2 FREE gifts (gifts are worth about $10 retail). After receiving them, if I don't wish to receive any more books, I can return the shipping statement marked "cancel." If I don't cancel, I will receive 6 brand-new novels every month and be billed just $4.55 each for the regular-print edition or $5.80 each for the larger-print edition in the U.S., or $5.49 each for the regular-print edition or $5.99 each for the larger-print edition in Canada. That's a savings of at least 11% off the cover price! It's quite a bargain! Shipping and handling is just 50¢ per book in the U.S. and $1.25 per book in Canada.* I understand that accepting the 2 free books and gifts places me under no obligation to buy anything. I can always return a shipment and cancel at any time. The free books and gifts are mine to keep no matter what I decide.

Choose one: ☐ **Harlequin Presents®**
Regular-Print
(106/306 HDN GNWY)

☐ **Harlequin Presents®**
Larger-Print
(176/376 HDN GNWY)

Name (please print)

Address   Apt. #

City   State/Province   Zip/Postal Code

Mail to the Reader Service:
IN U.S.A.: P.O. Box 1341, Buffalo, NY 14240-8531
IN CANADA: P.O. Box 603, Fort Erie, Ontario L2A 5X3

Want to try 2 free books from another series? Call 1-800-873-8635 or visit www.ReaderService.com.

---

*Terms and prices subject to change without notice. Prices do not include sales taxes, which will be charged (if applicable) based on your state or country of residence. Canadian residents will be charged applicable taxes. Offer not valid in Quebec. This offer is limited to one order per household. Books received may not be as shown. Not valid for current subscribers to Harlequin Presents books. All orders subject to approval. Credit or debit balances in a customer's account(s) may be offset by any other outstanding balance owed by or to the customer. Please allow 4 to 6 weeks for delivery. Offer available while quantities last.

Your Privacy—The Reader Service is committed to protecting your privacy. Our Privacy Policy is available online at www.ReaderService.com or upon request from the Reader Service. We make a portion of our mailing list available to reputable third parties that offer products we believe may interest you. If you prefer that we not exchange your name with third parties, or if you wish to clarify or modify your communication preferences, please visit us at www.ReaderService.com/consumerschoice or write to us at Reader Service Preference Service, P.O. Box 9062, Buffalo, NY 14240-9062. Include your complete name and address.

HP20

THE CHRISTMAS ROMANCE COLLECTION!

10 FREE BOOKS IN ALL!

'Tis the season for romance!
You're sure to fall in love with these tenderhearted love stories from some of your favorite bestselling authors!

YES! Please send me the first shipment of three books from the **Christmas Romance Collection** which includes a FREE Christmas potholder and one FREE Christmas spatula (approx. retail value of $5.99 each). If I do not cancel, I will continue to receive three books a month for four additional months, and I will be billed at the same discount price of $16.99 U.S./$22.99 CAN., plus $1.99 U.S./$3.99 CAN. for shipping and handling*. And, I'll complete my set of 4 FREE Christmas Spatulas!

☐ 279 HCN 4981   ☐ 479 HCN 4985

Name (please print)

Address   Apt. #

City   State/Province   Zip/Postal Code

Mail to the **Reader Service:**
IN U.S.A.: P.O. Box 1341, Buffalo, NY 14240-8531
IN CANADA: P.O. Box 603, Fort Erie, Ontario L2A 5X3

---

*Terms and prices subject to change without notice. Prices do not include sales taxes, which will be charged (if applicable) based on your state or country of residence. Offer not valid in Quebec. All orders subject to approval. Credit or debit balances in a customer's account(s) may be offset by any other outstanding balance owed by or to the customer. Please allow 3 to 4 weeks for delivery. Offer available while quantities last. © 2019 Harlequin Enterprises Limited. ® and TM are trademarks owned by Harlequin Enterprises Limited.

Your Privacy—The Reader Service is committed to protecting your privacy. Our Privacy Policy is available online at www.ReaderService.com or upon request from the Reader Service. We make a portion of our mailing list available to reputable third parties that offer products we believe may interest you. If you prefer that we not exchange your name with third parties, or if you wish to clarify or modify your communication preferences, please visit us at www.ReaderService.com/consumerschoice or write to us at Reader Service Mail Preference Service, P.O. Box 9049, Buffalo, NY 14269-9049. Include your name and address.

XMASRI9

INTRIGUE

Available December 17, 2019